This is a work of fiction. Names, characters, places, and incidents either are the product of the author's imagination or are used fictitiously. Any resemblance to actual persons, living or dead, events, or locales is entirely coincidental.

First paperback edition 2024

Anuci Press edition 2024

www.anuci-press.com

Cover Design by Ruth Anna Evans

ruthannaevans.com (google.com)

ISBN 979-8-9914345-5-3 (paperback)

ISBN 979-8-9914345-6-0(eBook)

POISON IVY (A PREQUEL TO NANA) & OTHER...

CONTENTS

I'm dedicating this book to my father, Michael Thomas Towse, who has just gone into full-time care. A victim of dementia, his time in the real world is hazy and fleeting at best. It's hard to watch a man who could once hold a room disintegrate in such a way—a horror story in its own right. I owe him so much, including my strange outlook on life and twisted sense of humour. This one's for you, Dad! Anyhow, I hope people enjoy this story and the bizarre characters in the manner intended. We are all just kids trapped in adult bodies, but with the realisation that time is not as abundant as it first seemed. Feel everything. And laugh. Laugh until you double over with tears in your eyes.

Poison Ivy: A Prequel to Nana

Chapter One: What is Love?

A Cheap 'n Cheerful shopping bag erratically hurtled across the otherwise deserted streets. The rain kept most town folks inside, flickering boxes behind closed doors offering more inviting worlds full of colour and perfect smiles. According to the weatherman in the shiny suit, there was to be no let-up for at least six weeks. "Time to search the shed for the Scrabble board or a jigsaw puzzle," he'd said in the previous day's transmission, following up with his perfect smile. But at the bottom of Newhaven Crescent, beyond the faded 'Missing' posters stuck to lampposts that spilled out dirty yellow light, Nana Ivy was trying to reassure Clementine it was perfectly reasonable to run a knife across her husband's neck.

"I can't do it. I can't!" Clementine screamed. "I have to go. The chicken needs defrosting for tomorrow night."

Ivy clamped a crusty hand around Clementine's. "He's prepared to give up; let you die, Clemmy. If he truly loved you, he'd be willing to try anything to keep you alive."

"He does love me. He's just—he's just—"

"Happy sitting on his fat arse, watching The Price Is Right? Sending you to the post office to pay bills while cancer eats you from the inside out."

"But the doctors said there was no hope. It's why they sent—"

"Do you trust me, Clemmy? Do you?"

"I don't know. I just don't know anymore." Clementine started to sob, her left leg buckling, forcing her to use one of the handles of the wheelchair for stability. "I feel funny, and my head's spinning. And what about the chicken?"

"It's the only way, Clemmy."

"What did you put in that tea? Can't think. Can't—"

"The only way."

Body trembling, Clementine studied the lady she'd met at the post office less than a few weeks ago. Her first impressions were of a friendly old woman, one with a spark behind her eyes and exuding a compelling energy that made her want more. Smitten, she'd have gone so far as to say. "You and your husband should come to the community centre for one of our jamborees." Ivy had said. "A proper knees up and a great bunch of people."

She'd been excited, a chance to get out of the house, thinking it might give her and her husband a second wind. "Not a chance," Alf had said. "Bad enough I ever catch sight of my reflection; I don't need any more reminders of how close to death I am." A stubborn old fucker stuck in his ways and mostly to the armchair with the visible head grease running across the top of the fabric. "Put the kettle on, will you, and stop being so daft."

Yet, enamoured by Ivy's charm, Clementine had agreed to meet the nice old lady for coffee, soon finding herself divulging her deepest and darkest secrets, things she'd never told another soul. In return, Ivy had captivated her with tales of recovery, ones that lingered in

Clementine's head long after Alf had turned the lights out each night. Sceptical for sure, but intrigued, nonetheless. Janet, Geoff, Albert, Benjamin, and Harry—just a few of the names she could recall. "I took their pain away, and I can take yours away, too," Ivy had said, vague about the details but sincere with her delivery. "We're a proper family, prepared to do what it takes to keep each other alive. But it must be both of you; we have no room here for stragglers. All in or all out."

And so, when the pain had become almost unbearable, and needing to know if there was something to all Nana Ivy's tales, Clementine had dragged her husband to the community centre on the false pretence of free food and beer and watching the match on a big screen TV.

The woman in front of her, though, looked harsher than the one she met in the line that day, intimidating. "Clemmy, stop crapping and get cracking!" The necklace pendant draped between Ivy's heaving breasts pulsated a blurry red, and Clementine was sure she could feel the sting of heat.

"Ivy, I—" Pressure on her hand, Clementine winced as Ivy helped guide the blade towards Alf's throat. She could not deny that on occasion, she'd had thoughts of driving one of her knitting needles into the old fucker's saggy neck, but that was a far cry from actually doing it. For better, worse, richer, poorer, in sickness and health, to love and to cherish, until parted by death. The very solemn vow.

"You'll be rid of it once and for all. Free of the poison that riddles you."

The community centre suddenly smelled different to Clementine, staleness, piss, and detergent replaced by something even more noxious. She looked down to see the first bead of magnificent red leaking down her husband's contrastingly pale skin. It wasn't her idea of a jamboree, far from it, not a single mince pie or glass of sherry in sight.

"He's my husband, Ivy."

"But he isn't prepared to listen, Clemmy, more concerned with getting back for the game than trying to help his dying wife."

"But the things you said." Mumbo jumbo, as Alf had whispered under his breath to her. Made up voodoo stuff, all that talk about sacrifices and offerings for the sake of more time. The woman's off her bloody tree.

"Survival instinct, Clemmy. It's always been this way. We're just doing what it takes to keep breathing."

"It's wrong, though. Can't you see that?"

"What's the alternative—withering away in a hospital or some dingy bedroom? Taking sustenance from a straw while someone wipes our arse, lying through their teeth by telling us how much better we're looking? It gets my goat, I tell you. Not good enough, Clemmy. Just not good enough. Below par. SUB-FUCKING-STANDARD!"

Clementine recoiled, Ivy's voice still ringing in her ears. "He's my husband," she repeated. "And the chicken; I need to—"

"When was the last time he said he loved you?" Ivy said in a much softer tone.

The claws of pain had relented a little, an enticing reminder of what life was like before stage four cancer. Likely the effects of the drugged tea, three Nana Ivy's now stood before her, all with their eyebrows joining to form a V-shape.

"Go on," Ivy said. "When was the last time?"

She could feel herself beginning to sway, the room starting to spin around the chair's wheels. The only time she could remember feeling so out of it was the weekend away with the girls. Somewhere on the coast. Where was it again? And that guy with the slick-backed hair and crooked nose, chasing after her like a dog on heat. "I'm married," she'd told him, rejecting his advances. But she'd secretly enjoyed the attention, already beginning to feel invisible to her husband.

"Clementine!"

She recoiled again, feeling herself drifting in and out of reality. "Can't remember. Nineteen-eighty-five, I think, after Everton won the football."

"When was the last time he made you a drink? When was the last time he bought you a birthday present?"

"I don't know if he's ever made me a drink," Clementine replied. "He bought me a set of trowels and gardening gloves for our last anniversary and some non-stick pans for my seventieth."

"Jesus wept. When was the last time he gave you a good seeing to?"

"Huh?" She scrunched her face as though someone had just asked her to explain the theory of relativity. "Oh, that. Nineteen-eighty-five, after Everton—"

"For the love of Christ!"

"Please. I just want to go home. The chicken, Ivy!"

"It's him or us, Clemmy. We're all dying, every last one of us, and only you can save us."

"That's not fair. It's too much. I just want to—"

"Do it," Ivy said, eyes suddenly bulging, face all twisted. An abscess on her face gave a gentle crack, a puff of black dust emerging. "Too late to back out now. He won't be happy."

Clementine couldn't take her eyes off the black treacle-like liquid that had started to spill down Ivy's cheek. Nothing made sense anymore. She opened her mouth and closed it again, wincing as another lesion on Ivy's face exploded, sending a spray of dust into the air and stickiness across the old lady's face and down her flowery blouse.

"DITHERING REALLY GETS MY FUCKING GOAT!" Ivy screamed, her grip tightening around Clementine's, the pendant flashing more intensely than ever.

A million thoughts ran through Clementine's head, but none provided clarity. She scrambled through her mind's dark and foggy alleys, searching for moments of happiness, but each one offered only a dead end or underlying bitterness. Why wasn't her husband prepared to go to any lengths? Wasn't that the true definition of love? Decades together, but how many of those years counted? How many reached beyond servitude or the sheer numbness of sitting in front of the goggle box?

Darkness coursed through her; she could feel it in her veins. Voodoo stuff. She put up a fight but had little of it left. Whatever was inside her was staking its claim, confusing her moral compass and wooing her with thoughts of being pain-free. Ever since Ivy had mentioned the possibility, she'd been unable to shake the desire for release. But that was just a dream. Just a lot of mumbo jumbo.

"For the greater good," Ivy muttered. "For the greater good."

The words bounced in Clementine's head with increasing intensity. As if she was under some form of hypnosis and going deeper every second, the compulsion to repeat them grew stronger until it became overwhelming. "For the greater good," she said. "For the greater good. For the greater good." The pressure on her hand finally relented, although Clementine could still feel Ivy's hold. "For the greater good."

"Welcome to the flock," Ivy said.

She couldn't open her eyes. Wouldn't.

"You're one of us now. Part of something truly special."

Clementine let the knife slide from her hand, flinching as the clamorous racket offered a gritty reality to an almost out-of-body experience.

"You'll never feel alone again, Clemmy. We're an extension of you, a union, a hive mind intent on survival. We are love, and we are life."

She finally allowed herself to look down. If it weren't for the blood leaking from his neck and pooling against the leather, it would just be like any ordinary evening; her husband slumped in a chair with his mouth hanging open. "Oh, Christ. What have you done?" she said, turning to Ivy, the old lady's face full of renewed warmth and compassion.

"We, Clemmy. We. Always we from this day forward." After dipping a finger into Alf's wound and then suckling on it like a newborn baby on a teat, Ivy finally offered a smile. "He will be happy."

Clementine snapped her head to the left, sure that she saw movement. "Have to get back for the chicken." The smell of mould and piss became overshadowed by something far stronger, a rotten pungency that turned her stomach. She tracked a shadow moving along the wall but could not find a source. "The chicken." They were no longer alone; she knew that much. Someone else had come to join the knees-up.

From behind, Clementine heard a door open, a rabble spilling into the room. Before she could turn, her legs finally gave way. Lava-like blobs of darkness swam around the outside of her vision until, one by one, they joined. "Likes his chicken, does my—"

Chapter Two: We'll Meet Again

As Clementine dug her fingernails into the arms of the chair, laughter floated across—a crackly yet childish giggle that didn't seem quite right. And something else, a nostalgic sound that evoked memories of her school days, sitting quietly for assembly while one of the classes tried to get through their performance as quickly as possible.

Maracas?

To another eruption of mocking jeers, Clementine snapped her eyes open to see a strange man with googly eyes parading up and down a makeshift stage, rattling what looked to be a lunch box.

"Alright, sit down, Geoff," someone shouted from the front of the room. "You're already over your five minutes and boring everyone shitless."

Dropping his shoulders, Geoff breathed heavily down the microphone and flipped everyone the bird before marching off stage. "Don't fucking need this."

Still feeling in a dream-like state, Clementine followed the pounding of footsteps to track a small overly tanned man wearing a bright yellow suit onto the stage. The guy looked like a matchstick; a misshapen reject tossed on the pile. "Let's hear it for Geoff," he said, bringing his stumpy hands together, a huge microphone clasped in the right. "He might be shit, but at least he turns up every week."

"Hey, I've got feelings, you know."

"But zero fucking talent," someone mocked.

"Okay, okay," Rodney said. "Now, if I can have your full attention, as today is a very special day, ladies and gentlemen."

"Why's that Rodney?" someone at the front yelled. "Is Edith keeping her clothes on for once?"

"Oi, I've still got it," Edith retorted, puckering her lips.

"You haven't even got your own teeth, love."

"Some things are better without teeth," she replied. "As you well know, Harold."

Ear-piercing wolf whistles filled the room as the tiny blue-haired lady simulated the act of fellatio, sticking a tongue into her cheek and bringing her knobbly fist backwards and forwards towards her mouth.

"Alright. Settle, please." Cheeks flushing with even more colour, Rodney began tapping the microphone frantically, eyeing the crowd and waiting for the residue of disruption to fade. "Without further ado, I take great pleasure introducing a new member to our fold this evening. And our beloved leader has informed me she has quite the voice."

Another lonely wolf whistle filled the room, followed by a shout, "Get on with it, you piss-mop!"

Rodney twisted his face and gave the crowd a look that could kill. "Please join me in welcoming Clementine onto the stage."

Heads began turning until the room was just an ocean of teeth and eyebrows. Hairs prickling on the back of her neck, Clementine squeezed down harder on the arms of the chair, but it wasn't enough to prevent the shudder running down her spine at the sight of the gas mask on table nine, its wearer offering a wave that failed to console her.

"Come on now," Rodney said. "Hands together. Let's give her a really warm welcome. Make her feel at home."

Rapturous applause spread across the room, followed by chants of her name. Through the haze, Clementine ran her eyes across the people closest to her, the glass in front of her trembled as they all began drumming against the table. A man with a scruffy beard immediately to her right looked beyond excited, face turning as red as a beetroot, one of his eyes looking like it might pop out at any second. When it did, Clementine was sure she'd pass out again.

"Albert, for the love of Christ," a woman behind him said. "Can't you do something about that?"

"Only if you do something about that mouth of yours," he replied.

"Clementine! Clementine! Clementine!"

She began shaking her head, but the chants only got louder. As Albert fumbled between her legs, looking for his eye, she finally caught sight of Ivy on a table towards the front, lips moving, eyebrows knitted together. The invasive fog that had filled her head was beginning to dissipate, realisation crashing heavily down that her husband was no longer of this earth and that she'd just signed up for a place in the nut house. "What have I done?" she muttered. "Oh Christ, what have I done?"

"I can't find my eye," Albert announced from under the table. "Can someone help me find my foo-king eye?"

"Clementine! Clementine! Clementine!"

Ivy's eyes remained fixed on her. We, Clemmy. We. Always we from this day forward. The old lady offered a stern nod, suggesting participation wasn't optional.

"I need my eye!"

"Calm down, Albert. Use one of the bingo balls for now."

The noise escalated. Gums got bigger; eyes got wider. An almighty squeak emerged from a table to her left, Clementine tracing it back to a white-haired lady with a puppet draped across her arm. "I can't take you anywhere," the lady said to the puppet, all colour drained from her face.

"Clementine! Clementine! Clementine!"

She could feel Ivy's eyes still burning into her but dare not check. Focussing on the glass that continued to move across the table, she wished for nothing more than to be back in her living room, the TV playing loudly to itself, competing with Alf's snoring.

"She loves us, you know," the rotund lady to her right yelled into her ear. "As if we were kin. Perhaps more. We're a family now."

Clementine instinctively smiled but shifted in her seat.

"The name's Janet," the woman with the buzz cut continued, offering a giant hand.

Instinctive courtesy overriding discomfort, Clementine reached for it, left in dismay as Janet pulled the colossal thing away and offered a salute instead. "You better get up there, love. Dithering really gets her goat."

Clementine put the noticeable lack of pain that usually ransacked her body down to whatever Ivy had put in her tea. Or shock. Even as she got to her feet, using the table to support her weight, the usual ferocious stabbing across her back was nothing more than a dull throb. Still, as she straightened, she grimaced, ready for the inevitable surge of agony.

You'll be rid of it, Clemmy, once and for all. *I wouldn't be here today if it weren't for this necklace.*

Just mumbo jumbo, Clem. Let's go home and put the kettle on.

I'm so sorry, Alf.

Finally, she let go of the table and took a small step, her face still twisted in anticipation.

Nothing. Not a twinge.

She took a second and more confident stride. And a third. And a fourth. No longer tentative, Clementine marched confidently towards the stage, unable to stem the feelings of euphoria at being able to move so freely and painlessly. *I'm sorry, Alf. I'm so sorry.* After countless years of suffering and enduring arduous hours of treatment, it felt like she was floating, carried by rapturous applause that filled the room.

"Clementine! Clementine! Clementine!"

She marched past Ivy's table, making eye contact, this time the lady offering the same warm smile she'd given in the post office. *She loves us, you know.* She noticed Ivy's cheek, which had only recently erupted a gooey blackness, now looking unspoiled and radiant.

"Nice tushy," someone hollered as she mounted the stage.

"Keep your hands on the table, Harry," someone retorted.

Taking a deep breath, Clementine grabbed the microphone. *I'm so sorry, Alf. Sorry. So sorry.* She wiped a tear from her cheek and turned to face her crowd.

"Show us your tits!"

"Seriously, Harry, we'll make you walk around the block again."

"Go on. Just lift your dress so we can see your nip-nips."

"Harry!"

The room fell to silence, the chanting finally coming to an end. Clementine swallowed hard, running her eyes over the hungry audience. It had been a day and a half, but not one to tell the grandkids about, first running a knife across her husband's neck and then taking part in a talent show for the walking dead. Ivy smiled at her, offering another encouraging nod. They gave me six months, Clemmy, but that was seven years ago.

She brought the microphone to her lips, jolting as a crackle exploded across the room, finally giving way to her go-to song of yesteryear. She swallowed hard. "This one is dedicated to my—to my late husband, Alf." The words brought more tears to her eyes, but professionalism countered as she launched into the first line of 'We'll Meet Again.'

It began as a tentative performance, her voice competing with the guilt that gnawed at her insides, not helped by further calls from Harry to get her knockers out. By the time she arrived at the verse, though, she was strutting across the stage like a diva, back in her comfort zone, back to the pubs and clubs where she once brought all to tears. She moved gracefully and freely, losing herself in the music, feeding off the crowd's attention. Soon, there wasn't a murmur among them, all stares directed towards the stage, hanging on her every word.

Even after she sang the last line, the crowd remained silent, their stares fixed towards the stage as if in an almost hypnotic state. Finally, the music died, giving way to several sniffles around the room and an ever-so-gentle knocking sound.

"Harry, stop that right now!"

But the thrumming only intensified, accompanied by the faintest of grunts.

"Harry!"

Emerging from the haze of performing, Clementine lifted her gaze towards a scrawny little man, his left hand gripping the base of the chair, his right ruffling the impossibly white tablecloth around his lower half. His eyes were teary and bulging, his face twisted and puck-ered.

"Will someone please get him out of here?"

"I'm not going near the fucker in that state. He bit Bruno on the arm last week."

After a series of moans and pig-like squeals, the knocking finally stopped. The old man slumped back in the chair, his face unravelling as he reached for a serviette. "That was wonderful," he said, turning his stare to Clementine. "You were wonderful."

It finally became all too much for her. Overwhelmed, Clementine dropped her microphone and marched off stage towards the ladies, avoiding eye contact with all, especially Harry.

"You're a fucking disgrace, Harry." someone shouted.

"Was it something I said?"

"A truly wonderful performance," Rodney announced as another song crackled across the room. "Now, we're going to have a short break. Bars open, though, so—"

As the bathroom door shut behind her, Clementine began to sob. An image of Alf invaded her mind, blood spilling down the white shirt she'd only ironed a few hours previously. "What do I have to wear that for?" he'd said. "I can't enjoy my jellied eels wearing that thing." Letting the wall of the nearest cubicle take her weight, Clementine slid to the floor and buried her head into her hands. She bit her lip, the smell of detergent filling her nostrils as she sniffed back more tears.

"Mumbo jumbo," Alf had said.

But Ivy's skin. And the undeniable feeling right now that she could trip the light fantastic. What kind of black magic—voodoo stuff—was this?

A tap at the door startled her. She swallowed hard and remained quiet.

"Clemmy, let me in."

She recognised Ivy's voice, but sure as shit, she wasn't ready to face her.

"I just want to talk. Like we used to, Clemmy."

"You tricked me; put something in my tea."

"Only courage. Courage to fight. Courage to put yourself first for once."

"Alf's dead."

"Alf died a long time ago, and you know it. He was killing you, too. But we're fighters, you and me, Clemmy. It's why you came today. It's why you allowed the knife to glide across his neck."

"That's not true." But as more tears came, Clementine wasn't sure of anything anymore. "Not true."

"Tell me how your body feels, Clemmy. Let's talk about how nice it is to move about without nauseating pain running through our bones."

Habitually grimacing as she stood, Clementine observed herself in the mirror opposite. Even through the tears and smeared mascara, the lack of pain carrying in her face was evident. Colour was in her cheeks, frown lines not as prominent, her posture projecting the woman before cancer took hold.

"Clemmy, I just want to talk."

"This is wrong. It isn't how things should be."

"Why not? Why shouldn't it be? All those years of subservience and living to please others for what? We're not even seen as real people anymore. I refuse just to roll over and die. It gets my goat, Clemmy."

"What about the chicken?" She didn't even like chicken. In all those years of eating at the same table, Alf hadn't noticed she had never even touched the meat on her plate.

"This will take time, Clemmy, but I saw you on that stage, how your face lit up when the music started. And your movement, how elegant and graceful it was. Embrace it. Look upon this as another chance to find yourself, a second wind away from the shackles of a lifeless marriage."

She hated to admit it, felt unclean even thinking it, but deep down, buried under layers of morality, part of Clementine was already beginning to embrace the freedom. Not just the blissful escape from pain's grip, but grief and guilt aside, the prospect of not being at someone's beck and call from morning until night.

"You can sing and dance as much as you like, Clemmy. You'll always have an eager audience here. And bring the rest of the family; we'll have a right good shindig."

A shudder ran down Clementine's spine at the prospect of performing again. She'd felt like a million dollars on that stage, even with Dirty Harry's shenanigans. Alf wouldn't even allow her to sing in the house. "I can't enjoy the bloody music with you singing over it," he used to say. And as for family, the miserable bastard had no time for anyone. "Bunch of fakes, sniffing around for their inheritance."

"Let me in, Clemmy. Come on."

Even the dampened music trespassing under the door sent her skin prickling—another song from the unmistakable Vera Lynn. Wiping the moisture from her face, she slid up the cubicle wall and started mouthing the lyrics.

"Clemmy, please."

After tidying her snow-white hair in the mirror, Clementine opened the door to Ivy's warm smile and a flurry of music and chatter. "I want to know everything," she said, holding back more tears. "And then I want to sing again."

Chapter Three: Council Offices (Six months later)

"You've really got the short straw with this one, Si."

"Yeah, yeah, so I've been told. New kid and all that, I guess." He picked up the file and gave it a flick through before sliding it into his briefcase. "I've dealt with a lot worse than a bunch of excited pensioners before, Rach, so forgive me for not shaking in my boots."

"Jacob did more than that. He moved across the bloody country. Rumour has it, he's changed his name to Beatrice and lives in a campervan somewhere."

"Don't believe everything you hear, Rach. According to Beccy on reception, Flynn from accounts has three nipples."

Rachel smiled. "How do you know he hasn't?"

"Cos, I made the bloody thing up."

"Bastard."

"Only because he called me a four-eyed creep at the last work-do. Hey, have you thought any more about drinks tonight?"

"I'm still considering it." Offering a smile, she started tapping the keys on her PC. "You know my situation."

"Just drinks."

"Don't pressure me; it's a turn-off."

"Well don't blame me if I end up running away with one of the old dears from the centre." He grabbed his jacket from the stand and headed towards the door. "I bet some of them still have some gas in the tank."

She laughed. "Oh, plenty of gas, I reckon."

"I'll send you a postcard from Florida."

"Good luck."

"Don't need luck." He wrapped his fingers around the handle and gave it a confident yank. "Old people love me; they'll be putty in my hands."

"That's what your predecessor, Jacob, thought," he heard her say as the door closed behind him. Old people love me. Old people love me. What kind of a boast is that, you silly bastard? "Morning, Trevor."

Trevor looked at Simon as though he'd just slapped him on the leg with his dick. "I need that report on my desk first thing."

"Yes, boss." Prick.

"Don't come back empty-handed. Insist your way in."

"Yes, Trev—I mean Trevor." Fuckwit.

The rain was refreshing, washing away the staleness of the office. Lifting his stare to the clouds, Simon stuck his tongue out, longing for the day he could tell Trev where to stick the job. "Pissant. Rectum. Ass licking chair-sniffer." The guy was looking for an excuse to get rid of him; that was the rumour around the office. And how he'd been skulking around Rachel added some rare validity to such gossip. Dirty old bastard, breath like a rotting corpse. Fucker should just retire and prepare for death.

He let his tongue linger before getting in his middle-of-the-road car and heading towards the community centre. He didn't mind driving, a chance to get away from the office and work through the plot of his next horror story. That was his passion, what he thought about when he woke from restless slumber to when his head hit the pillow again. His recent piece was about a guy from middle management called Trevor, the big reveal being that the guy was on probation from Hell for being a dick, tasked with hitting his quota for misery-making before being allowed back in again.

"Get in the right lane, you cock!"

Thoughts turned to Jacob as the windscreen wipers squealed. In his experience, there was rarely smoke without fire, only if he happened to be rubbing the gossip sticks together. But just to move town after an afternoon with the crusties? There had to be more to it, Simon thought. Either that or the old fuckers were holding him captive, making him empty nappies and read out bingo numbers on request.

"Where did you learn to drive, fucker? Helen Keller Driving Academy?"

Rachel. Lovely Rachel. Always going for the bad guys: Muscled freaks covered in tattoos, head shaved, glasses-free. He didn't get it. Granted, he wasn't Chris bloody Hemsworth, but he'd been known to make a head turn or two. Usually older women—older women love me—but still. And she was so confident and intelligent, wasted at the council. Maybe that was it, some self-destructive streak, or perhaps—

"Asshole! Use your fucking mirrors."

Anyway, he didn't want to give Trevor an excuse to get rid. He'd be even less appealing jobless, and his mission was to make her his, short of shaving his head and tattooing her name across his pecker.

"Get off the road, you crazy old fuck!"

Bloody crusties. If he could get past the inevitable smell of the centre, he thought, they'd be putty in his hands. He had an innocent look about him that appealed to the older generation, the glasses helping. And there was always so much concern for how skinny he appeared. "You need fattening up, love. Nothing but skin and bone," his ex-girlfriend's grandmother used to say, making it her mission to force-feed him, thrusting some freshly baked item towards his face every time he crossed the threshold into her house. "A strong gust of wind would sweep you away, laddy." And she frequently provided said blast, often letting rip in front of the open fire and unintentionally stoking the flames.

"Open your fucking eyes, you muppet!"

In and out, that was the plan. He was just doing his job. Somebody else would be doing it if he wasn't. And he didn't have to tell them anything. Christ, he figured he could say what he liked, and the poor old fuckers would believe him. "Yes, I'm your new bingo caller. Number sixty-seven, stairway to heaven." Aside from number one, Kelly's eye, that was the only other one he could remember from when his nana used to drag him to that room full of teeth and nostril hair. "Yes, I'm your entertainment for the evening. What do I do, you ask? Sing? Juggle? Certainly not but watch me fill out this report and shut you fuckers down quicker than you can say 'Where's the muscle spray?'"

As Simon fought back his guilt, rain pelted at the windscreen. The new shopping centre was coming, and he could do nothing about it. Progress was inevitable; people were living longer, ergo the town required more infrastructure to support everyone. It wasn't his decision but came from the bigwigs upstairs. He was just tasked with submitting the report, paving the way for so-called progress.

"Get off the fucking road!"

The change of pace was welcome as he got off the highway, finally turning into Newhaven Crescent. Nobody behind him, he slowed the car, taking in the surrounds that again gave him flashbacks to when he stayed with his nana—tiny houses with giant chimneys and cracks running across cobbled pathways leading to doors with frosted glass. The moment caught him off guard, even bringing a tear to his eye.

"Can of Coke and a Mars bar for you in the cabinet, pet," she used to say. The promise of such a sugary overload should have made him giddy, but the drink was always warmer than tepid, and the chocolate never failed to exhibit a strange, white coating. It reminded him of those rare sightings of white dog turds, always making the eating experience less pleasurable. He recalled the tight blankets, endless bowls of soggy cereal, and the piss-stinking shaggy toilet mat that never failed to make him queasy. As if this new memory conjured an accompanying pungency, he quickly wound the window down, allowing a pleasant and nostalgic smell of baking into the car. Tidy flurries of colour emerging from countless hanging baskets added a tinge of sweetness, taking him back to his nana's garden, her big knickers always hanging from the washing line, occasionally catching on the breeze like yacht sails.

"Rest in peace, Nana."

Curtains twitched as the car crawled along, his stereo crackling and irrationally making the hairs on his neck prickle. Seeing what looked like a gas mask poking through dirty yellow nets, he leaned forward, chin almost resting on the steering wheel. "What in the name of—FU-UUUUUUCK!" He slammed the brakes on hard, jolting forward.

Only a few feet ahead, the cat planted itself in the middle of the road, seemingly unperturbed and staring him down.

"Have you got a fucking death wish, cat?" Heart still thundering, Simon offered a non-Doctor-Dolittle-approved gesture of both middle fingers. "Go on then, move it." He lightly tapped the horn, but the cat still showed no reaction. "Pssst. Go on; fuck off!" The haunting figure in the window was long gone, but the black moggy seemed ready for the long haul. "Just a fucking cat." But he hated them.

His nana used to have one that smelt worse than her toilet mat, little dried bits of shit always trapped in the hairs around its asshole. It was a rescue cat that she'd decided to call Graham. Anyhow, shitty-arsed Graham always used to seek him out, planting himself in his lap and making a meal of it. With what could only be described as a frown, the cat used to stare up at him, protracting and retracting its claws as if daring him to move. The one time he did, the fucker turned into the female equivalent of Cujo, hissing and clinging onto his crotch, refusing to let go even as the scared young boy performed hip thrusts Tom Jones would have envied. Left and right, it swung, ears pinned back, eyes carrying a threat of sneaking into his room after lights out and scratching the skin from his face. Nana Judy later admitted that she'd wet herself from laughing so hard.

"Fuck off. Just fuck off."

The stand-off at the bottom of Newhaven Crescent continued for what felt like an eternity, Simon offering several light toots of the horn, the cat giving its own version of the middle finger. Finally, with complete disinterest, it looked away, licked its paws several times, and began sauntering towards the house at the far end. Simon watched the cat squeeze its fat arse through the iron posts of the gate and finally come to rest on the doormat, pricking its ears when he started rolling the car again.

"The feeling is mutual, cat. You can sit there looking superior and proud, but at least I don't spend hours on end licking my genitals." He'd tried often enough as a kid, but that was none of the cat's business, and he was a much rawer version of the person he was today.

Newhaven Crescent Community Centre, the sign on his left confirmed. More patches of planted colour did their best to help brighten up the building centred in the middle of a glorified wasteland, the monochrome sky and crumbling pavements more accurately setting the tone. Lending assurance that his journey would not be a waste, a morsel of dirty yellow light escaped from one of the side windows.

After parking between two faint white lines, he checked himself in the mirror and collected his briefcase. "Like taking candy from a baby." Patience was vital with old people; he knew that much. Deep down, he also knew they just wanted to connect, to feel something other than redundancy. Being overly fond was part of that, almost a clumsy regression to childhood methods of reaching out. That's why he sometimes allowed Doris from number seven to slap him on the arse. "Cheeky," he'd say to her. But if she ever tried to slip him the tongue or grab his pecker, he'd likely throw up in his mouth and never leave the house again.

Straightening his tie again, knowing old people were suckers for formal attire, he cleared his throat and prepared to knock on the door. He took a deep breath of fresh air, knowing it was all downhill from thereon in.

CHAPTER FOUR: THE POWER OF THE DARK SIDE

<u>Benjamin</u>

After placing the walkie-talkie back on the coffee table, Benjamin picked up another matchstick and dipped both ends in the small puddle of glue. Holding his breath, he did his best to keep his hand steady, but the arthritis was already back with a vengeance. "Fuck it to Hell and back." Two-thirds finished, the model replica of The Colosseum was his best yet, but he'd only managed a handful of matchsticks all week and not a single one that day. "Where's the fucking force when you need it?" he said, following with, "You don't know the power of the dark side," in his best Darth Vader impression.

That dozy prick, Alf, had bought them a little more time, but things were getting worse again. The boil on his neck had erupted like a volcano, its stickiness pooling at the back of his mask, not to mention the one on his backside that had grown yet another head. Time was running out; hard decisions had to be made. But sometimes, fate played a hand, Benjamin thought, rubbing his hands together, careful not to break the skin again. And the lanky streak of piss that had just parked outside their precious community centre was a royal-bloody flush.

Giving up with the model, he put the matchstick down and removed the mask, examining the glistening pink goo across its base. "Never say die." He moved his hand to his face, running it across scar tissue that was beginning to open and weep again. Even after all this time, his fear of death was undeniable, but Nana Ivy had never let them down.

"It's going to be a good day."

Excitedly, he rushed to the bathroom, prising off the shirt that had begun sticking to his back. Next were the pants, a slow process that never failed to open the puss-filled lumps decorating his thighs. Grimacing, he peeled away his underpants, unable to bring himself to look down, making that mistake last week and getting the fright of his life, his manhood resembling a mutated and bloody baby's finger.

The shower was always a bitter-sweet experience, one he mostly squinted through, trying to avoid the sight of the blackish viscosity that swilled in the tray beneath him. After several minutes, he grabbed a towel and gently patted at his skin, finishing up by laying some dressing across the worst of the openings. Another shudder of adrenaline rattled through him as he headed to the bedroom and opened his closet.

"Time to shine."

Running his eyes over his collection of lustrous shirts, he began singing the lyrics to 'Stayin' Alive,' performing a half-assed hip thrust he immediately regretted. More hairs prickled at the back of his neck at the thought of the impromptu get-together and what the day would bring. Deciding to go all out, he opted for green flared pants and the rainbow-striped shirt with pearlescent buttons, completing the outrageous look with his blue suede loafers. Not forgetting the gas mask, of course, the perfect complement to any outfit, especially if your skin resembled shredded cheese.

"Looking good, Benji. Looking good."

Now it was just a question of feeling good, he thought. Recalling the days of his youth when life had seemed infinite, he sprayed himself down with cologne from arse to ear and back again. All the days tossed away like chips on a poker table, and here he was, trying to milk each one for everything it had, survival instinct turned up to the max.

Ivy had saved him, no doubt. Losing Betty, his wife of over fifty years, had transformed him into a shadow of himself. And when cancer took hold of him not long after, the entire family had appeared from the woodwork, assuming it was just a matter of time.

But death was subsequently put on ice when his friend Janet visited with Ivy in tow. Not only removing cancer from his bones, Ivy gave him a reason to go on, a family even more loyal than his own. He owed her everything; he owed them everything.

And he intended to pay back every last bit of debt.

The walkie-talkie offered a crackle in the other room, prompting Benjamin to gently rub his hands with glee again.

Chapter Five: So Far, So Good

"Hello?" As Simon closed the door behind him, the smell immediately made its presence known. It was even worse than expected, a musty and oppressive cocktail of mould and piss that immediately made his eyes water and his stomach churn. Instinct screamed for him to escape, but he knew the sooner his checks were complete, the quicker he'd be on his way.

Don't come back empty-handed.

He ran his eyes across the centre's deteriorating state, already noting half a dozen red flags. Flaking layers of different coloured paint adorned the walls, and to his right, there was a crack about half an inch wide that ran from ceiling to floor. "Like taking candy from a baby." An untidy montage further along the same wall caught his attention, wooden boards giving beneath his feet far more than he felt comfortable with as he moved closer to investigate.

Next to a faded floor plan, at least two dozen photographs of old people lined the walls, accompanying names written across the bottom. "Edith. That's a very cheeky smile, Edith. Harry. Geoff. Nice peepers, Geoff. What you looking at, Willis? Janet. Vee. Albert. And—what the fuck?" He pushed his glasses further up his nose, but the gas mask was undeniable. "Stone the fucking crows." His eyes had not deceived him earlier, after all. "Benjamin, smartest of the bunch."

Afraid the smell would stick to him if he hung around too long, he finally slid the paperwork from his briefcase and clicked his ballpoint pen into action. Just as he was about to scratch his first cross at the very top of the list, more shuffling emerged from his left. "Hello?" He held his breath, not sure if he wanted a reply. "Hello. Is someone there?"

Nothing.

"Suit yourself." After filling the first five boxes with an X, he moved through the corridor, finally arriving in the main room and shaking his head at the sight of the unlit and cracked 'Fire Escape' and 'Emergency Exit' signs. "Naughty. Naughty. Cross. Cross." The smell was just as noxious, a little less pissy, but more like rotten eggs, precisely what he imagined Hell to smell like, albeit further tarnished with the scent of burning flesh.

"Who the hell are you?"

Simon turned, instinctively hugging his clipboard to his chest as he surveyed the googly-eyed fellow clutching the lunch box. "I'm Simon."

"Are you today's act? Benji said it was going to be a good one."

"Benji? The guy in the gas mask?"

"Yeah. Do you know him?"

"No."

"So, who are you?"

"I'm Simon."

"Nice to meet you, Simon; I'm Geoff." The old man offered a bark, holding a hand in the air as he reached into his pocket with the other. "Excuse me." He pulled out a bloody handkerchief and brought it to his mouth just in time to catch a series of violent convulsions.

Simon watched helplessly. He wasn't good in emergencies, remembering when his microwave set on fire. Frantically trying to fill a sieve with water was the first red flag, the second being the well-known fact that water and electricity don't mix at the best of times. "Are you okay?" he asked, feeling immediately silly. No, the poor fucker obviously was not okay. Eyes red, bulging, and tortured breathing between his hacks, Geoff looked on the verge of pegging out. "Should I call someone?" Simon said, his follow-up question at least a little more proactive.

The old man shook his head, finally lowering the handkerchief and revealing a congealed mess resembling several squashed slugs. Momentarily, Simon thought he saw a pulse in the centre of the glistening mass but put that down to his anxiety.

"I'm Geoff," the old man said.

"I'm Simon." Patience was vital. "Nice to meet you, Geoff."

"Are you today's act, Simon? A comedian? A juggler even?" The old man's smile grew impossibly wide, and his watery eyes all but sparkled. "Don't tell me you're a magician? I bloody love magicians."

"I'm afraid not; I'm from the council."

"Is that a band?"

"No."

"Oh." The strange man offered a rattle of the lunchbox and took his place on the back row. "Only Benji said it was going to be a good one."

"I'm sure it will," Simon said, offering his polite smile. After scribbling down two more Xs, he headed towards the bathrooms, holding his smile as the cock-eyed wrinkly tracked his movement. On the way past, there was an impossibly strong compulsion to grab hold of the crazy old fucker's head to try and shake his eyes back in place.

"Do you know Benji?" the voice crackled from behind. "And what did you say your—"

As Simon quietly shut the bathroom door behind him, a new form of torment emerged from the far cubicle. He felt the blood rushing from his head, his feet tingling as though unable to cope with the flurry.

"Well, hello there, stranger," the old lady said. "You really should knock, though."

Simon froze, swallowing hard and doing his very best not to throw up. "This—this is the gents."

"Ooh, silly me." The hunched-over and naked old woman returned to her business, humming a tune as she continued scrubbing at her crusty inner thighs with a toothbrush, rivers of watery blackness carrying flaky skin down her pasty pins. Offering the gummiest smile, she raised her stare. "Do you want a picture, love?"

Oh, God. Oh, Jesus. He recognised her from the photographs, the one with the very cheeky smile. He spun around and reached for the door handle.

"Just teasing. I'm Edith. What's your name, handsome?"

"I'm—I'm Simon," he replied, wishing for the ground to swallow him whole and for God to strike him with temporary amnesia.

"Needn't worry about the pins, love. My stockings would snag if I didn't get rid of the worst of it. Give it a few hours, though, and they'll be like two drainpipes, ready for all the rats."

"Right," he said. "I'm going now. Bye, Edith."

"Something I said, petal?"

The door closed behind him, but he knew the image would be forever imprinted on his mind. And that God-awful scrubbing sound.

"Do you know Benji?"

Simon lifted his gaze to the googly-eyed freak and his lop-sided smile. Unable to take any further onslaughts of madness, he focussed his attention back on the paperwork. Only a few blank boxes left; he'd be out of the place in a few minutes, sniffing up the petrichor, the rain washing away the uncleanliness.

"Only Benji said it was to be a good un."

Any more room in that fucking campervan, Beatrice? Offering a shudder, Simon made his way towards the corridor, determined to finish the job and not to give Trevor the benefit of calling HR.

"Are you a magician?"

If I were, the first thing I'd do would make you disappear, you crazy old fuck. It had turned into one hell of a day, the only chance of a reprieve if Rachel accepted his invitation for drinks. Chances were slim based on the number of times she'd declined, but something in her eyes at the office had suggested she was on the verge of caving. He'd call her later, trying to entice her with tales of the loons, although likely steering clear from the part about Edith raking at her front bum with a toothbrush—hardly a mood setter.

"I like magicians," Geoff sang from behind, rattling his lunch box.

Fuck off. Fuck off. Just fuck off. Simon upped his pace to a march, filled with the anticipation of escaping the centre and thoughts of stepping into a lovely warm shower driving him forward. Old people love me. Old people love me. But something felt off about the ones he'd met so far. This bunch seemed all curdled and sour, like milk left in the sun too long.

He kept his stare dead ahead, eyes on the door at the end of the corridor. With nothing on the map to indicate there should be a room there—floor plan violation—his curiosity was piqued. With every bone in his body, he hoped there'd not be another crusty standing behind it, scrubbing at their nether regions.

Less than halfway down, more scratching to his right pricked his ears. He paused, examining the sign that read 'Storeroom.' As he stretched an arm out towards the handle, the scuffling sound intensified, making him think twice. Rats. The health and safety jackpot. But as he twisted the silver knob, a shadow moved under the door, prompting him to recoil and let out a garbled rasp. The folded piece of paper that emerged through the gap took his anxiety to a whole new level.

"Rats. Big fuckers, too."

Heart pounding, he turned to see a well-built lady carrying a broom in her left hand. "I'll sort it," she said, offering a salute with her right. "Janet Hinchcliffe." Feeling like a first-class prick but unable to stop, Simon reciprocated the salute, the words 'Simon Cosgrove reporting for duty, Ma'am' on the tip of his tongue. "Simon. Simon Cosgrove."

"Did you get everything you came for, Simon?"

"Huh?"

"For your clipboard."

He swallowed hard, searching for the correct response. "I think so. Just boring work stuff, you know." His words came out too fast, running into each other. He felt irrationally nervous, a bead of sweat running down his cheek. "Not what I'd rather be doing. Not my passion."

The woman twirled the broom, revealing several flaps of blackened skin hanging from her arm. Not only that but as she started shuffling towards him, he saw something pulsating on the side of her neck. "And what's that, Simon Cosgrove? What's your passion? What floats your boat?"

He took a small step back, placing his right foot onto the crumpled paper. Unable to take his eyes from the rhythmic throbbing of whatever was attached to Janet Hinchcliffe's neck, he swallowed hard. "I—I—"

"Well, spit it out, love! Has the Devil got your tongue?"

Floorboards creaked impossibly loudly as he shuffled backwards, his heart upping its tempo. "Horror. I write horror." He dropped his pen to the floor and crouched to retrieve it, discreetly pinching the note beneath his shoe.

Janet smiled, the changing tension in her face prompting the boil to give birth to something dark. "Horror, eh?" she said. "Try getting old; that's a living fucking nightmare, Simon."

Simon took another long step back, the creak of the boards sounding louder than ever. What the fuck? What the geriatric fuuuuuuck? The small globule of black that now rested on the lady's left shoulder offered a pulse, prompting the skin to shrink around Simon's skull. "There's—there's something on your shoulder," he said, sliding the note into his pocket.

"Things that go bump in the night? Monsters?" The woman slotted a key into the storeroom door and yanked it open. She twisted her face and shoved the broom end into the darkness, prompting another loud scurry and then—silence. "I find real life much more terrifying, don't you?" She slammed the door shut, locked it, and then turned to face him, the blob offering another pulse as something crawled from its guts. Finally, the burly woman looked down and gave whatever it was a nonchalant brush from her shoulder.

No longer on autopilot, Simon forced himself to breathe, unable to believe his eyes as he took several wobblier steps back. His chest contracted as the alien object took to flight, buzzing manically around Janet's head. "But we go on, don't we?" Janet said, appearing oblivious. The worm-earwig-fly hybrid emitted a wet squeal as it darted in and out of the air between them. "Taking what pleasures we can."

Simon's mind screamed for him to run for it, to somehow force himself past the leathery quarterback standing between him and fresh air. But instead, he simply stood there, visions of his legs crumpling beneath him if he tried. Grotesqueness continued its clumsy aerobatics as Janet approached, still wearing that smile and effortlessly twirling that fucking broom.

"I—I must be going now," Simon said hopefully. "Paperwork, you know."

The thing finally fell to the floor between them, offering a high-pitched squeal as it flapped its tiny wings and writhed, legs kicking redundantly in the air. Janet's giant right foot came down heavy, ending its short but manic life with a sharp crunch, her smile fading.

At the sound of a doorknob turning, Simon spun around, the vein in his head pulsating perfectly in time to his thundering heart. A short woman with weeping cheeks offered a smile and a festering arm, a chequered blue and white tablecloth bunched over something in her hand. "What's your favourite pie, petal?"

Simon observed the whites of what he assumed to be a pie dish poking from beneath the cloth. "Huh?" The familiar smell of fresh baking filled his nostrils, but unlike before, it filled him with dread over nostalgia. His dear old nana wouldn't have said boo to a goose, but this woman looked deranged, eyes wide and manic, a smile splitting her face and most of the sores that decorated her pallid skin. "Your favourite pie," the old woman repeated.

He was well beyond being able to rationalise anything that was happening at Newhaven Crescent Community Centre. He'd stepped into something old and smelly and felt like he was sinking fast. His chest tightening, Simon watched a trickle of watery blackness work down from the woman's left nostril to a groove in her chin. A darkened tongue emerged from her thin lips and lapped it away, only for another river of even darker fluid to begin its journey.

"Sweet or savoury?" Simon finally managed to croak.

"We're all about sweetness here, Simon."

He didn't even recall telling the woman his name, but figured it wasn't the time or place to bring it up. More patches of skin prickled as he alternated his glance from the tablecloth to the crazy old bitch with the melting face. Why did it feel like a test? Oh fuck. Fuck. Fuck. Another bead of sweat trickled down his back as he considered his answer.

"Well?" The woman scrunched her face up in an obvious sign of impatience. "I'm asking for your favourite pie, not the capital of Turkey."

Ankara. He knew that one as it had come up in a pub quiz a few weeks ago. Insisting until he was red in the face that it was Istanbul, he looked like a prize plonker when the answers were finally revealed. That said, his friend Nancy was convinced the coccyx was—

"Waiting!"

Simon recoiled, his mind drawing a blank. Suddenly feeling like a child in her presence, he couldn't even remember the last time he'd eaten something that hadn't come out of a microwave. "Er—"

Pie. Pie. Pie. What are the fucking different types of pie? Rhubarb? Pear? Is that a pie? Pear pie? Can't fucking think. What's wrong with me?

He could see the urgency in the woman's eyes as they all but popped from her head. Why did she terrify him so much? Just an old dear who discovered moisturiser and self-care far too late. But what about the bug that flew from the big fucker's neck?

"Dithering really gets my goat," the old woman warned through gritted teeth.

It was a last warning; he knew it. Before what, though? Something told him his punishment would be more than a pie in the face or drawn-out tales of yesteryear. On the verge of tears, an outing with his father flashed through his mind. An American-style diner had opened an hour's drive away; it was the talk of the town. All the servers dressed in funky American gear, or at least, the stereotypical version the British owners had conjured up. "Key lime." He remembered looking through the glass casing, and turning to his dad, hungrier than he could ever remember. "That's my favourite pie! Key lime pie with a big dollop of cream, if you fucking please."

His smile faded as the old woman's face twisted to a grimace. She began to cough, body wrenching and convulsing with each violent hack. Something splashed onto the floor between them, offering a gentle wriggle before falling through a crack in the wood. "How dare you!" she rasped. "How bloody dare you!" She offered another series of barks, looking on the verge of keeling over. "Janet, did you hear what filth emerged from the young man's lips?"

"Shocking, Ivy," Janet replied. "Truly shocking."

"If you love America so much, why don't you just fuck off and marry it?" Nana Ivy clenched her fists, veins as dark as night threading through her arms. 'Key-lime-fucking-pie. Mercy be."

"I'm sorry. I'm sorry," Simon said, feeling like his collar was constricting around his neck. "It was just the first thing that popped into my head. Can I have another go?"

Face puckered, eyes narrowed, Ivy offered a growl and an imperceptible nod.

Simon swallowed hard, still mystified as to why he felt so damn terrified. But then he remembered that some poor fucker was locked in a cupboard. "Okay. Okay. Then it has to be... apple. Yes, apple!"

Ivy snorted, offering an exaggerated shake of her head. Simon felt like his insides might drop out.

"No. No wait," he said. "One more try, okay? Okay? It's—It's—"

Holding out her other weathered hand before her, Nana Ivy began shaking her head, seemingly all out of patience. "Gets my fucking goat," she said under her breath. Something dripped from her chin onto the floor that she quickly turned into a dark smear with her right foot. "Janet, is it too late or do you think we can convert him?"

"I'm pretty sure we can, Ivy. Nothing comes close to your cherry pies."

"Very well," Ivy said, offering a wink to her friend.

Cherry? Cherry pie? Cherry? And pie? Feeling like he'd just been cheated out of the gameshow jackpot, Simon turned but couldn't get his hands up in time to stop the broom end finding his skull.

Chapter Six: A Big Day

Clementine's fingers ached as she guided the eyeliner pencil across. Even the simplest things had again become fraught with difficulty and inevitable discomfort. She moved onto her lips, gently smacking them together after doing the best job possible with the bright pink lipstick. Ivy's request. It was to be a big day, an old-fashioned knees-up, and people were to dress in their best for the occasion. "Opportunity had come knocking," she'd said.

As she stepped away from the mirror, she took in her reflection, her posture stooped and her lined face wearing the relentless agony that once again explored every part of her. A series of boils lined the right side of her cheek; they were new. Makeup could only do so much, and the poking and prodding around only made them angrier, some projecting warm jets of disgust onto the towel wrapped around her.

She knew what they were doing was wrong. Yet, the urge to feel pain-free again, as agile as the singer that took to the stage the same night as helping end her husband's life, was undeniably strong. Ivy had explained it all, using her undeniable charm to make the whole thing sound as natural as evolution. Guilt was still raw, but this was Clementine's "extended family," and she "had a duty to them now." The stuff in her tea, Ivy had said, only accelerated fate. You trust me, Clemmy, don't you?

Biting her lip to stem the tears, Clementine brushed a hand through the clothes in her wardrobe, pausing on a glittery strapless dress she couldn't ever remember wearing. She held it against her, tempted to do a twirl but knowing the pain would likely bring her to her knees. She let the towel drop and tentatively dressed, giving herself only a cursory glance in the mirror when done. On the way out, she grabbed her sparkly heels to match, almost crying at the thought of slipping into them.

Grimacing with every step, she slowly descended the staircase, still unable to get used to how empty the house felt. It was far too big for her, especially as the grandkids had no interest in staying anymore. "She smells like wet cardboard," she'd overheard one of them say. And deep down, she knew looking after the kids provided the sole motivation for a visit from her daughter and son-in-law. It was well before Christmas she'd last seen them, and that was only to drop the presents off on the way to a function.

"Someone else will get it if you don't act fast," Nana Ivy had said about a place up for sale near the community centre. She guessed she probably would take it.

The taxi was already there when she reached the bottom of the stairs. "A big day, especially for you, Clemmy," Ivy had said. Wondering what that meant, Clementine slipped on her heels and stepped out into the rain.

Chapter Seven: Handbags and Gladrags

As Simon began coming to, he could hear Rod Stewart's gritty voice playing over a boisterous rabble. He tried to moan, but something across his mouth kept his lips from parting. His head thrummed, offering a flashback to the wild look on Janet's face as she brought the broom into his skull. Finally, he opened his eyes, offering a sharp inhale and jolting upright in the wheelchair, restraints tightening around his chest.

What the—

Only a morsel of light sneaked through drawn blinds, aided ever-so-slightly by a candle at the centre of each table, tiny flames casting flickering shadows against the neatly piled stacks of red books. Profusely blinking as if it would help, Simon lifted his gaze from the table.

Oh, fuckity fuck.

The place was full of them, wall-to-wall crusties with leaking skin and knobbly growths, some pulsating, some just oozing. More glistening redness awaited in a white dish in front of him, surrounded by thick golden pastry. Beer, pie, and piss provided a potent concoction of smelling salts, but something even stronger churned his stomach and helped snap him back into the twisted reality. Rotten eggs?

"Youngster's awake from his nap," a voice to his right said. Simon traced it back to a man he recognised from the montage, only with what looked like a ping-pong ball squashed into his left eye. No, not a ping-pong ball, a fucking bingo ball. Easy mistake to make, he guessed. Number one: Kelly's eye.

"Just in time for the show, handsome."

He lifted his gaze, the blur finally settling to reveal Edith holding a pint glass towards him. She wore a rather elegant purple satin dress, the image of what lurked beneath still far too fresh in Simon's mind. At any moment, he thought his brain might snap. I want to go home. But the yarn around his wrists, legs, and chest provided little hope.

Old people love me. Old people love me.

His struggles became more urgent, his mind beginning to flood with thoughts, none rational. Gums, teeth, and glistening sores awaited whichever direction he looked. Far from the days that he could recall as a child when he occasionally accompanied his nana to bingo, there was a different look in the watery peepers that burned into him now, one of hunger, one of savagery.

"What do you want?" Simon yelled through the makeshift gag.

The crowd mocked him, imitating the kazoo-like noise and drumming on tables like over-excited school children. As Edith walked towards him through the crowd, Simon began working himself into a frenzy, veins popping as he tried futilely to free his hands.

"It's jumbo weight yarn, that is, lad." He snapped his head to the right to see the big lady—Janet Hinchcliffe—the one who thrust the broom into his skull. "You'll not get far with that."

"I'm ready for pudding," someone shouted. "Where's my pudding?"

Edith finally arrived, offering a grimace as she leaned in towards him. She ran a scaly hand across his cheek, her cloudy eyes offering a sparkle. "Oh my, your skin is so soft. Soft as a baby's bum-bum."

Jumbo weight yarn? A nostalgic fucking nightmare! He felt like he was drowning in madness, each of the fuckers well past expiry and stark raving bonkers. He offered another incoherent yell, the thrumming in his head escalating towards an explosive crescendo.

"What's up, handsome?" Edith twisted her face as she straddled him, something cracking on the way down. "You've seen the menu, and now you're ready to order?"

Cheap perfume and a strong smell of liquorice made him feel sick, but the thought of her thighs on his finally prompted a bit of vomit in the back of his mouth. Make it stop. Please make it stop. But another round of wolf whistles kicked off as Rod Stewart launched into a new number, his crackly voice floating across from the bar. Edith responded to the crowd, beginning to writhe against Simon, raking herself up and down his legs with something beyond pleasure registering on her face.

Simon scanned the crowd, hoping someone would step in, but only leers and jeers greeted him. Even the puppet appeared excited, bouncing up and down on its owner's leg until the woman covered its eyes with a scaly hand. "You've got your hand up my arse," the puppet said. "I think we're past all that."

"I WANT MY PUDDING AND I WANT IT NOW!"

Music only seemed to get louder. Faces floated in and out of vision, cruelly making him think he was on the verge of passing out. Fucking gas mask. The nightmare levelled up as Simon noted his brand-new pants covered in skin flakes, the contrasting wetness against his thigh prompting another gag.

"A bit of wee," Edith cried joyfully, riding him like a wild buck. "Just a bit of weeeeeeeeeeeeeeeeeeeeee."

And, just like that, the music died, and Edith removed herself from Simon's thigh. To the sound of footsteps from behind, he strained his neck to see the stern old woman—Ivy—emerge from the room that wasn't on the map. The place was silent, the crowd beginning to part as jerkily as Edith's legs, making way for Ivy as she stoically marched towards the stage area. Everyone began taking their relevant places, a more dampened but palpable excitement gripping the room.

Momentarily, darkness swallowed them. And that smell, getting stronger all the time. What the fuck is that? Simon began searching the room, but his attention turned sharply back towards the stage as Ivy offered an impossibly loud clap of her hands. Almost immediately, something round and yellow appeared in the corner of Simon's eyes, the madness continuing as a rotund and excitable man, face as red as a slapped arse, brought the microphone to his lips. "Testing." A subsequent high-pitched squeal filled the room, causing an immediate backlash from the crowd. "Testing."

"Test this, motherfucker," someone yelled, holding a wonky middle finger towards the stage.

"What the fuck, Rodney?"

"Sorry. Sorry," the host said, his face red as an airway beacon. "Is that any better?"

The crowd grumbled. Edith flicked her head back towards Simon and offered a wink.

"Get on with it, Rodney. I just want my pudding."

"So, a bitter-sweet occasion this evening," Rodney said, stare aimed towards the floor. "In our heart of hearts, we've known it's been coming, but I'm afraid it's time."

Murmurs filled the room. Some of the old fuckers began to sob and comfort each other, passing handkerchiefs and napkins around until the sniffling finally faded out.

"I know, I know," Rodney said, still with his chins squashed against his chest. "For the greater good."

"For the greater good," the crowd chanted sombrely.

"He's been a great dog, providing plenty of entertainment, brightening our days, and putting a smile on our faces. I think we'll all miss him; I know I will." Rodney wiped a tear from his cheek and offered a loud sniff down the microphone. Not a heckle from the crowd. "We've waited as long as possible, but Alf's passing only bought us a little time. Fate has played its hand, and it's finally time to make the offering."

Simon's wrists burned, but he was making progress, feeling some give in the wool. An offering? What the fuck are these loons up to? He gritted his teeth, trying to force a hand through the gap, momentarily distracted as the room fell again into temporary darkness as though a cloud was passing over.

"And if we're being honest, we all know old Jay hasn't been looking too well of late," Rodney continued, "not himself at all. It's the kindest thing to do."

"Kindest thing to do," the crowd chanted.

Rodney nodded, offering another sniffle. "Very well then. Let us eat pie and then commence."

Simon thought back to Rachel's words. "You've really got the short straw with this one, Si." There was the short straw, and then there was this. It's only a cult! A fucking crusty cult with animal sacrifices and all. Doing his best not to break down, he struggled against the wool, trying not to draw attention from the others. He was nearly out; just one more—

A giant hand ripped off the tape, causing his mouth to ignite. Offering a cry, he lifted his head back as far as the chair would allow, only to see his old friend Janet standing behind him, offering a salute with her other hand. "Time to eat your pudding, soldier." With that, she leaned over, wrapped her meaty fingers around the crust of his pie, and thrust what she could into his open mouth. Before Simon could even consider what was happening, Janet had stepped behind him, covering his mouth and pinching his nostrils. "Swallow."

Already, his lungs were exploding. He shook his head like a rabid dog, but her vice-like grip wouldn't give, the sheer size of her bloated hands not allowing even a smidgeon of air through. From all directions, he could hear moans of approval and the sound of spoons against dishes.

"Swallow," Janet yelled sharply.

"Pudding! Pudding! Pudding!"

The pastry was initially sharp against his throat, but the warm filling provided delayed lubrication. Once again, it conjured snapshots of evenings spent with his nana, but she'd never grinded her body against him or shoved her fist down his throat. That wasn't the sort of thing a nana did. A spot of knitting or watering their plants, perhaps, but never in a month of Sundays would they scrub their fannies with a toothbrush or try to choke you out.

"Good boy," Janet said softly, finally removing her hand.

He swallowed a little more, allowing himself to breathe freely. Cherry. It was cherry. None out of ten for service, but he couldn't deny it was an easy ten for flavour. Like nothing he'd ever tasted before, even from his own nana.

"None of that key lime, rubbish," Ivy shouted across. "Proper pie with a proper filling. And it has to be fresh cherries, not tinned."

"Fresh, not tinned," the crowd concurred.

Simon took in some more air, wondering what the fuck was going to happen next. It was like being on board a never-ending fairground ride, not allowing him to catch his breath before the next big plummet. His lips were going numb, and there was a strange tingling sensation across his limbs, all of which he put down to the restraints. But when the room started spinning and heads began to float, he suspected there might be more to the celebrated pie than just fresh fruit.

"And now," Rodney said, clearing his throat, "before we get to our main business, we move to the talent show part of the evening. Only a handful of acts today as Albert still can't find his eye, and I know many of you are feeling a little under the weather."

"Fucking understatement of the year," someone shouted. "I think I shit out a kidney this morning."

"So, without further ado," Rodney continued professionally, "let's hear it for Liz."

The crowd groaned to their feet and began to erupt, a domino effect of applause and farts, even a possible shart from Maud on table number seven. "Excuse me, one moment," the old dear said. "Nature calls."

Simon thought there was nothing natural about what was happening around him. Believing he saw something against the wall to his right, he snapped his head around. Nothing. And again, darkness to his left. And ahead. To the right. But it was as though he was just missing it each time, whatever it was. Panic gripped him, but also an undeniable and bizarre urge to ask for more pie.

What the fuck is happening?

With the dummy dangling upside down from her arm, Liz shuffled towards the stage, the biggest grin on her face. She moved carefully, obviously in pain but with an overwhelming urge to be the centre of attention. Or at least not invisible.

"Break a leg, Liz!"

"I'll break yours if you say that again," the dummy answered, causing a ripple of laughter. "And the name's Terrence. Liz is the one with her hand up my arse, the kinky bugger." Something dropped out of her dress as she mounted the steps. It offered a wet squelch and a high-pitched squeal that might have caused Simon to pass out if he hadn't already witnessed the events from the corridor earlier. Only a dampened snigger left his lips as the thing gave an audible pop, leaking its darkness into the wood. "Fucking old people," he muttered.

Without saying a word, Liz sat on the barstool and balanced the dummy on her knee. She ran her eyes across the crowd, milking the feeling of importance, of being more than just another pissy inconvenience. Her eyes clouded with tears until she blinked them away and swivelled the puppet's head to face her.

"Have you been drinking today," the puppet said.

"I might have had a couple of gin and tonics. Why?"

"Might explain why you're talking to a fucking puppet."

Liz turned to the crowd, jaw dropping open with fake surprise. "How rude."

"Mind you," the puppet said, "I had a few last night. Ended up sleeping under a car."

"Why did you sleep under a car?"

"So I could wake up nice and oily in the morning."

The crowd groaned but drummed on the tables as if hungry for more. Even with their eyesight, Simon imagined they could see the old lady's lips moving, but he guessed they were making the best of what they had. Has to be now. Has to be. With everyone's attention on the talentless old dear on stage, he let the yarn fall to the floor and offered another excited but stifled snigger. Three. Two. One. But his arms only wobbled like jelly moulds as he tried to lift them.

"My uncle died, you know."

Liz turned to the dummy with an exaggerated gloom etched across her face. "I didn't know that."

The puppet's head tilted towards the ground. "Yeah, he had a drink problem. Passed out after glugging too much furniture polish."

"I am so sorry to hear that."

"It was a slow death but a beautiful finish."

As more groans filled the room, Simon tried to work his arms again, but they were as useless as the puppet's. All he managed to do was draw attention from a white-haired woman on the opposite table, her boil-ridden face breaking into a sickening smile. "Hits like a train the first time," she said. "But you get used to it." The sympathetic smile widened further, causing the boils to erupt simultaneously, several fountains of orange spraying across the stark white tablecloth. Simon offered an involuntary and thunderous bark, sending the room into silence and heads spinning towards him, even the puppet's.

"I do believe our esteemed guest wants a turn," Ivy said, nodding towards Janet. "Let's see what he's got, Jan-Jan." The big lady smiled and stood, slipping a knife from the back pocket of her khaki pants. "I do love fresh meat," she said.

A bizarre concoction of fear and euphoria coursed through Simon as he aggressively shook his head. He imagined his eyes ending up pointing in different directions, the thought triggering another involuntary snigger. "You're all fucking nuts," he cried. "One sandwich short of a picnic." His suddenly high-pitched voice tickled him, accelerated further on seeing his old friend Geoff sitting two tables down, eyes like opposing magnets. "Only one oar in the water."

Simon guessed the blade in Janet's hand to be roughly six inches long. It looked half that in her giant hand. "Sit still, will you," she said, working the knife through the rest of the wool. Alternating between an overwhelming urge to laugh and a feeling he might piss himself with fear, Simon searched the room for a face that didn't advertise lunacy. Like looking for a knitting needle in a haystack, a black cat in a coal cellar, his hunt proved fruitless, only offering more curled lips, bulging eyes, and nipple-high pants. A disgruntled frown from the bald fella with a ping-pong ball for an eye finally sent him into uncontrollable hysterics. "Kelly called, you silly old bastard," Simon managed to croak in between wheezes. "Wants his fucking eye back."

"Oh, we've got a comedian on our hands, Ivy," Janet said. "This should be good. Better be anyway." Arms locked under his armpits, she hoisted him from the chair and dragged him towards the stage. "Wants his eye back," Simon repeated, prompting another solitary bout of tear-inducing laughter. "Save it for the stage, kiddo," Janet muttered. "You'll need the performance of your life."

"But what about me?" Liz said. "I haven't finished my act yet."

"She gets upset when she can't finish," the puppet said. "That's why she left her husband."

With a look in her eyes as though someone just took a giant shit all over her geraniums, Liz solemnly stood, her brief moment of visibility cut even shorter. "I could have been someone, you know," she said, shaking the puppet's head from left to right as she moped off the stage.

"You are someone, Liz," Harry offered softly. "A really shit ventriloquist."

"Fuck off, Harry."

"We can all see your lips moving, petal," Harry said, eyes lit up like a child's. "You need a longer skirt when sitting on that stool."

Liz went red and threw the puppet on the chair next to her. "Dirty bastard."

"And in any case, it was supposed to be my turn next," Geoff said, offering an aggressive shake of his lunchbox.

"And what was it to be this week, Geoff?" Harry asked. "Juggling? Unicycle riding? A bit of breakdancing? Or were you just going to rattle that stupid fucking tub of toenails like you do every week?"

"No, I was going to—I was going to—yeah."

After helping Simon up the small steps, Janet grabbed the microphone and held it to Simon's lips. Caught between a giggle and a scream, he studied the sea of blurry and manic faces. You'll need the performance of your life. A warm draught caught the back of his neck, causing a shudder to run down his spine. It all felt dream-like, soft edges, not straight, and something else, a feeling of—what the fuck? Another warm lick of his neck prompted him to snap his head around, darkness against the back shifting quickly.

"Clock's ticking, Simon," Janet whispered. "It's do or die."

Thinking he'd prefer Simon Cowell over this bunch of fuckers any day of the week, he swallowed hard, trying to make sense of it all. Old people love me. Old people love me. But that wasn't what they projected as they started drumming their spoons on the table. "Do or die. Do or die," they began to chant. He looked towards the exit in the distance, but it was as though he was viewing it underwater from the wrong end of a telescope. Besides, he had no faith in his legs to carry him more than a couple of feet.

"Get on with it, four-eyes," someone near the front shouted.

Fucking four-eyes again, he thought, but it somehow hurt more getting mocked by a pensioner. Darkness cast a shadow on his peripheral vision, but when he turned, it was gone. His heart thundered as another jet of warm air hit his cheek, bringing a stronger-than-ever feeling that someone—something—was in the room with them.

"Do or die. Do or die."

Always the comedian, it was his instinctive go-to, an extension of his insecurity. But that was down the pub with friends or when that gobshite Trevor was out of the office, not in front of an audience of the nearly dead with savagery drawn across their glistening faces. He began searching the crowd for material, his mind drawing a blank. "You know you're getting old when the candles cost more than the cake." Only one person snickered, but it felt more sardonic than sincere.

"You're shit, and you know you are," someone sang.

Simon snapped his head towards where the voice came from. "That was Bob Hope, for Christ's sake," he said. "What's wrong with you lot?" He looked towards Ivy, who folded her arms, a disapproving frown etched across her leaking face. "If there's one thing that really gets my goat," she said to the person next to her, "it's really shit comedians."

"Do or die," Janet whispered in his ear again.

"Wait! Wait!" Simon pleaded. Oh, Jesus. Oh, Christ. He needed something special, not something you'd find written inside a cheap birthday card. Think. Think! The heckling had tightened the invisible belt around his chest, and his shirt was damp from sweat. He cleared his throat, fingering his collar away from his neck.

"Jesus Christ," Harry shouted. "Can't we just put the fucker out of his misery?"

"I was standing in line at a cash machine the other day." Simon swallowed hard, hoping for a home run. "An old lady approached me and asked if I'd help check her balance." He monitored the hungry crowd, the punchline on his tongue. Fingernails dug into flesh. A bead of sweat ran down the right side of his face. "I pushed the fucker over and told her it was crap."

Heart in mouth, he ran his eyes across their stoic faces. A blurry shadow on the back wall loomed. His stomach churned, skin tightening around his skull. Whatever was in his system no longer cushioned the feeling of immense fear as he clung desperately to the microphone.

"Pushed the fucker over," an old dear from the centre of the room said. And in a delayed reaction that would have tested even the most experienced comedians, the crusties finally exploded into a subsequent guffaw. "Pushed the fucker over. Pushed the fucker over," was the new chant going around the room.

Seemingly out of harm's way, the shadow faded to nothing. His legs finally caved beneath him, and he slipped through Janet's fingers, collapsing in a puddle of piss and relief. "I think I've had an accident," he told his crowd.

"Join the club," someone shouted from the raucousness.

From the dusty stage floor, Simon watched Ivy unfold her arms. And was that a flicker of a smile across her face? She turned to Janet and shrugged, prompting the big lady to crouch towards him. He tried to raise his arms in defence, but only succeeded in slapping himself across the face. "Now, don't be a big baby," Janet said, dragging him by his feet, adding to his dizziness as his head played percussion on the steps. "You can relax now for the big finale." She hoisted him up back onto the chair, rearranging his limbs as though he was a puppet.

"I'm not a puppet," he cried, his body still not feeling like his own. He watched Janet waddle towards the corridor, wondering what the hell else the day had in store as a chain reaction of saggy elbows triggered murmurs from all directions. "I'm a real boy," he muttered, another involuntary giggle leaving his lips.

An impossible breeze sent the candle flickering violently, conjuring a noxious cocktail of urine, cheap scent, and cough lozenges. But something else, too, something Simon didn't want to spend too much time thinking about.

"I don't think I can watch," someone croaked from behind, following with a dog-like whine.

"For the greater good, Joan. For the greater good."

He watched Janet stop outside of the storeroom and reach into her pocket. Unarmed this time, she unlocked the door and stepped inside. "Stay," she yelled, prompting an uncontrollable snigger from Simon. Rats. Big fuckers, too. Finally, she emerged, dragging something behind on a rope. "That's not a fucking rat," Simon mumbled. He arched his neck, trying to get a better look over the 'hairdo' on the table in front, but his vision was still playing catch up, and the room refused to slow its spin. "What is it?" he said.

"That's Jay," Edith said. "The best dog one could hope for. Poor pup hasn't been well of late." She ran a wrist across her watery eyes. "The kindest thing to do."

"Kindest thing to do," the others repeated.

His arms redundantly banging against the base of the chair, Simon closed his eyes, counted to three, and opened them again. But no matter which angle he cocked his neck or how much he squinted his eyes, one thing was certain: The thing on the end of that lead had a goddamn motherfucking moustache.

"I'll miss that little bugger."

"Oh, Harry. You're just a softie at heart."

Janet got closer still, her hardened face temporarily washing over with a smidgeon of sadness. She sniffed loudly and gave the lead a lovable jiggle. "Come on, Jay. That's a good boy."

"Woof-woof."

The fever-dream feeling continued as Simon watched Janet approach the stage, Jay following behind, making his way up the stairs, long ears flopping and tail in a permanent forty-five-degree angle. It all suggested at least a modicum of happiness, but the lips above the moustache told of a contrasting misery. Janet turned to the dog—the man in the costume—and gave it—him—an affectionate pat on the head. Jay dutifully responded by sticking his tongue out and offering a series of excitable pants.

"In the name of horseshit," Simon mumbled, watching as a blue-hair 'from the table near the front slid a dish across the stage. "Here you go, Jay," blue-hair said with a croak. "A little treat for you." Jay sauntered over and buried his head in it, offering a series of loud chews and satisfied grunts. On all fours, he nudged the dish across the stage, trying to lick every inch of it clean. Fur smeared with filling, he finally lifted his head from the bowl, a half burp-half woof leaving his lips.

As another violent shudder worked through his otherwise redundant body, Simon reminded himself to breathe. "You're all fucking loco."

Jay snapped his head towards him, something beyond fear in his glistening eyes. "Woof." From what Simon could tell, the face beneath the fur was emaciated, pallid skin standing out against the brown. There's just no way. Just no way. But in his heart of hearts, Simon knew it to be true. Jay. Jacob. The dog approached the front of the stage, but before another bark or possible plea to a non-crusty could emerge, Janet put him in a headlock and dragged him to the ground.

Immediate and horrifying whimpers filled the stage, as did the sound of Jay's paws scuffing against the floor. Simon tried to get up, but his efforts were futile. "Stop this right now!" Unable to watch, he turned away, only to see the ominous shadow had returned on the walls to his left and right, this time far too defined for his liking and drawing ever closer. Horns, claws, and—"Make it stop. Make it fucking stop!"

"Clementine, you're up," Janet said breathlessly, her legs locked around Jay's midriff.

Clementine grasped the edge of the table but continued to sway. "I can't." She started shaking her head, her breathing becoming heavy and erratic. "I can't. I just can't." Colour in her face drained away until the tone of her skin resembled her snow-white hair. "Please don't make me."

"For the greater good. For the greater good."

"Clementine, you need to prove yourself to him," Janet said. "No assistance this time. You have to do it alone." Tears running down both cheeks and bloomers on full display, she continued writhing on the floor, locked tightly around Jay like a giant cobra. "Shh, Jay-Jay. It will all be over soon. Doggy heaven awaits."

"The kindest thing to do. The kindest thing to do."

"No, it fuck isn't," Simon cried, helplessly flailing his limbs. "The kindest thing to do would be to letter the fucker out of the headlock and get the poor bloke back to his family." Ivy offered a stern nod to the white-haired lady, prompting Clementine to stand. "You don't have to do this! You don't have to do this!" Simon screamed, but the sea of chants drowned his words.

With her head down and her body singing with agony, Clementine approached the stage. A big day, especially for you, Clemmy. She looked across to Ivy, who offered another nod, her face as serious as a heart attack. "For the greater good," the old lady mouthed. But nothing about what they were doing felt good to Clementine. She mounted the stage, grimacing as she bent over to retrieve the knife from a very red-faced Janet.

"You're all fucking mad," Simon screamed. "Bat-shit-fuck-ing-crazy!"

The chanting gave way to dampened cries and sniffles, a domino effect of grief that made its way around the room. More handkerchiefs stained with grotesqueness were again passed from table to table, cracking as they were opened, only to be filled with further vileness. Before long, the room was a symphony of blown noses, sobbing, and involuntary farts. "Oh, for fuck's sake," Maud said, shuffling off to the ladies again.

The shadow neared the stage, a long spindly figure with a jut-ting-out chin, its horns like antlers but appearing as sharp as knives. "You don't have to do this, Clementine," Simon croaked. "Please. Please stop." The white-haired lady looked at him, her face full of sadness and remorse. She opened her mouth, only a garbled croak emerging.

"Clementine," Ivy said. "Don't keep him waiting."

As if on cue, the shadow shifted to the back wall, an accompanying gust of warm air wafting through the room, extinguishing the candles and kicking up a smell that made Simon want to gag.

It all indicated the show was coming to a close.

Across the tables, people began reaching for one of the red books from the stack, hungrily licking their fingers and skimming through the pages. In a tongue unfamiliar to Simon, they began a new chant, wide and watery peepers alternating from the book towards the stage, where strangled yelps continued to emerge. Clementine dutifully crouched, her face exploding with agony on the way down, her moral compass broken long ago when she helped run a knife across her husband's neck. She was at the mercy of Ivy now, and she knew it. Putting him out of his misery. The kindest thing to do.

"Don't do it, Clementine," Simon yelled. He sensed weakness in her, some attachment to the real world that the rest of the fuckers had somehow lost. The white-haired lady's lips trembled, the knife shaking in her grip. "You're better than this lot; I see it in your eyes. Think about Jay. Think about—oh, no. Oh, Jesus fucking Christ, no!"

As Jay pawed at the knife protruding from his neck, Clementine stepped back, muttering something under her breath.

"You're truly one of us now, Clemmy," Ivy said.

Eyes wide with shock and pointed towards the ceiling, Jay kicked out several times, a series of watery gargles filling the room. Hope had betrayed the poor fucker, let him down in the most inelegant way. Simon could only imagine what the dog—the man—had been through.

"For the greater good. The kindest thing to do." All heads were pointed towards the stage, watching as Jay's movements slowed to nothing but an infrequent twitch, his breathing further laboured until it became a sort of half-choke-half rasp that curdled Simon's blood. In tears, Clementine collapsed on the floor next to him, stroking the fur on his belly as if trying to ease his passage into doggy heaven.

"For the greater good. For the greater good."

And after a final horrific choking sound, Jay—Jacob—was still.

"Bagsy on the toenails," Geoff yelled as if there was about to be a mad rush for them.

Heart in his mouth, Simon watched on as a smoky haze began to emerge from Jay's snout. Aggressively spiralling in on itself, the cloud made its way through the air, drifting towards the head of the shadow on the wall. As the crowd followed the trail, the chanting became even louder and more urgent, building towards a grating crescendo. And then, just like that, with a blinding flash of light and a thunderous bolt that shook the floor, the shadow and the haze were gone.

Silence.

Simon could not have imagined a more undignified death—dressed in a dog costume, being throttled by some poor dear with her knickers up to her armpits, then taking one in the neck from a white-hair for good measure. It would take some beating, for sure. And the poor fucker's last supper—leftover cherry pie from a bowl on the floor. Momentarily, he imagined Jay galloping through a field of sunflowers, barking with utter joy at being free from restraint and that darkened cupboard. It prompted an overwhelming fear that if he spent any further time with the lunatics, he'd end up just as demented.

"Let's get this party started," Harry yelled, all but jumping to his feet. "Music, maestro!"

"On it," Edith said, looking positively giddy. She moved quickly and gracefully towards the bar, a far cry from her performance when simply bending her legs had reminded Simon of dry kindling. "Pop or rock, Harry? What are we feeling?

"Horny."

"Give me a hand with the tables, Janet," Benjamin said. "My mask steams up if I over-exert myself."

Simon noticed the wound on Janet's neck was nothing more than a raised bump as she made her way over. And Ivy's face was no longer weeping, sores that once offered black ooze, appearing to be nothing more than age spots. What the hell is this happy horseshit? The more he surveyed the room, the more it became apparent the sacrifice he'd witnessed likely carried more weight than just an evil act committed by a bunch of stiffs.

"Let's have some Prince, Edith," a man with enormous ears shouted. "And make sure it's loud; you know I'm hard of hearing."

"That's not the only thing of yours that's hard," she replied, pointing a digit towards the tent in his pants. "Why don't you put your deaf aid in anyhow, you stupid old bugger?"

"Eh?"

"Never bloody mind."

Simon found himself wondering what their intentions were. Even with the fogginess still wrapped around his brain, he knew they'd likely not just let him walk out, not after having seen each of their weathered faces. Fuuuuuuuck! He didn't want to be an offering and certainly didn't fancy scrambling around on all fours, chasing after sticks and woofing on request.

With a crackle, the music kicked in, emphasising further the new-found agility of the members of Newhaven Crescent Community Centre's. Soon, only Simon was seated, watching the now makeshift dance floor fill with excitable geriatrics. Taking it as an opportunity, he thrust a leg out in front, but his arms collapsed beneath him as soon as he tried to propel himself forward.

Edith began twerking, much to Harry's amusement, who licked his lips and planted himself firmly behind her. "You sexy motherfucker," he cried, following her movement with his crotch area as best he could.

"Pace yourself, Harry," Edith said. "We've got all night."

"Don't worry about me, Edith. I've got more moves than a bowl of jelly."

It seemed grief for the passing of the beloved communal pet was ending, replaced by something that made Simon's stomach churn all over again. No boils or leaking gashes to speak of, but a new type of grotesqueness that looked to Simon like the beginnings of the world's crustiest orgy. He offered another groan as he tried to push himself from the chair, recalling a statement his mother once made, inciting that "all people over seventy should be put down." She was seventy-two now, showing no signs of expiry.

"Not now, Harry. Haven't you heard of foreplay?"

Never in a million years could Simon have guessed what the day would throw at him. Unable to stomach the Edith and Harry show any further, he turned away, only to see a woman with purple hair sticking her tongue down one of Norm's ears. "Oh, Norm. They're so big." Simon imagined her falling in, nothing but her wrinkly tights and ballet-style shoes emerging from the hairy darkness. Such thoughts triggered a giggle that he put down to whatever Ivy had put in that pie. He flopped his arms, managing to shuffle down the chair a little.

"Who wants a drink?" Albert said, spinning towards the bar. "Some lead for the pencil."

"The usual, Alby," people sang in chorus. "Easy on the ice," Edith added.

Simon writhed some more, his toes offering a tingle that slowly began to feed up his leg. At least it was something, he thought. Biting at his lip, he continued willing himself into the moment, fighting back the temptation to give to the relentless spin of the room.

"Hee-haw."

Simon traced the noise back to an old dear with smudged mascara. She was leaning over a table and getting dry-humped by Albert.

"Squeal like a piggy. Squeal like a piggy," he said.

"Squee, squee, squee," she responded, her face scrunched up to resemble a snout.

"Now do the sheep. Do the sheep."

"You're a baaaaaad boy, Alby. A baaaaaaad, baaaaaaad, boy."

"I am a baaaaaaad boy. Yeehah, motherfucker."

Simon refused to remain stationary, the tingling sensation upping its tempo. His body was slowly coming alive, an attempt to move the fingers on his right hand, bringing the middle one towards his palm. Come on. Come on! After several unsuccessful attempts, he finally managed to coil his fingers around the chair's base. Yes! The sensation of a million tiny spiders crawling across his skin spread from his hands to his arms and then shifted down his neck to his back. It was as though he was slowly defrosting or emerging from a cocoon. Biting at his lip and twisting his face, he raised his hand an inch above the armrest.

The music only seemed to get louder, as did the excited shrieks and thundering feet from the dance floor. Simon could only imagine what the escalating craziness might lead to. But he knew he had to bide his time, wait for the feeling in his legs and arms to return. Liquor was flowing fast, which meant two things: Things were about to get even more raucous, but also that his chances of escape would improve. He scanned the room again, beginning to think his mother had a point.

Edith had three blokes sniffing around her, thrusting, shuffling, and swaying. Each was red in the face and as though they were involved in some form of geriatric dance-off. The one nearest to Simon suddenly dropped to the floor and started 'doing the worm,' a move that seemed to take everyone by surprise. "Don't worry, gents," Edith reassured. "There's plenty to go around."

At the nearest table, Liz had the puppet under her dress. "Yes, Terrence, yes!" She writhed against the back of the chair, eyes almost rolling in her head. "Harry was right," Terrence responded. "I can see your lips moving."

On the other side of the room, Simon spied a tall bloke with a massive foot shaped like a boomerang. Just another freak for the collection. He watched the silly old fucker trip everyone up as he danced in an involuntary circle.

The music switched to something slow and sultry. Simon didn't recognise the song, but the cheers from the crowd led him to believe it was a favourite. In further celebration, the women unbuttoned their blouses, and the blokes began dropping their pants. Soon, the room was a montage of low-hanging fruit and soiled underpants. Make it stop. Make it stop. But on the contrary, things appeared to be just getting started.

"Neigh."

A horrible slapping sound followed the whinny to Simon's left. Even though he knew what awaited would be hellish, he instinctively turned to see Albert's pale saggy buttocks thrusting backwards and forwards. "Mooooooooooooooo," Joan sang, spread-eagled across the table, an impossibly large tuft of curly grey hair running up to her belly. "Hiss. Ribbit. Squawk. Squawk." Albert's doughy backside picked up velocity, his face twisting into something abhorrent, his breathing heavy and wheezy. Seeing the old man dry-humping Joan was scary enough, but this was a level beyond—a front-row seat at 'When Hairy met Saggy.' Yet, for whatever reason, he couldn't bring himself to look away, the scene mesmerising in the most horrific of ways.

Slap-slap. "Meow-meow." Slap-slap-slap. "Cluck-cluck-cluck." Slap. "Oink." Slap-slap. "Gobble-gobble."

It was finally Albert's turn to cry as he offered a series of violent shakes. "Owooooo," he sang, arms raised in victory.

Although Simon's hands still felt like balloons, they offered him a degree of control. His arms were no longer flopping redundantly but a few seconds behind doing what he wanted them to do. Come on! Come on! At some point, he knew the scenes beyond debauchery would end, and then what? He managed to curl his toes inside his shoes, but that was as far as it got with his lower half.

"Push it all the way in, Harold."

"It is! And I had a run-up."

Simon wasn't sure he'd ever be able to have sex again. The horrific sounds of marshy wetness, the laboured grunting, and the endless parade of pasty and saggy flesh would forever be etched on his mind. Closing his eyes didn't help; it only made him feel more vulnerable. As he continued moving his toes, he caught sight of Edith on all fours, taking it every which way and some. She snapped her head towards him and offered a wink and her gummy smile before returning to the wizened-up stick of jerky in front of her.

"Gobble-gobble," Joan said as she squatted beside her, eager for a turn.

Simon suddenly realised how stupid he was being. He was in a wheelchair, a chair with fucking wheels! He only needed his upper half, and if he could make it to the door, he'd be able to scream for help. Running his eyes over the four-wheeled relic, he felt charged with adrenaline. Where's the brake on these fucking things? At least it was something to keep his mind from the horrors surrounding him.

"That's it, Clemmy. For the greater good."

With renewed optimism, Simon gritted his teeth and worked his hand towards the lever near the wheel. Thoughts of fresh air and people with clothes on enthused him to giddiness. He had a plan. Not an elaborate one, but it was a plan. Chances are the old fuckers wouldn't even notice him wheeling away, all tangled up with each other. His eyes widened as his fingers brushed against the metal lever. Do or die. Do or die. But just as he was about to try and shift it, something cold and damp slapped against the right side of his face, almost sending the chair over.

"Oops, sorry, soldier," Janet said, removing a pasty white buttock from his cheek and regaining her balance. "Had one too many, I think."

Simon felt the cold wetness on his face long after she'd returned to the centre of the dance floor, caressing her breasts and running giant fingers through her lady garden. Fuck my life. Back to the job at hand, he managed to curl his fingers around the lever again. He felt some strength in his arms, too, able to twitch his muscles in a way he couldn't before. Knowing it could be his only chance, he took a deep breath in preparation, only to find three eyes pointing his way, Benjamin and Geoff leaning against the far wall, pleasing each other in 'gentlemanly fashion.' A strange sort of stand-off began, Simon's fingers on the chair's lever and theirs on each other's—come on, let me catch a fucking break, will you?

"Caw-caw. Caw-caw. ROAR!"

Unable to risk being spotted, he could only wait while Benjamin's mask continued to fog up. Scanning the rest of the room, he noticed Ivy on the far table, arms behind her head and eyes closed, the table-cloth ruffling either side of her. Got to be now. Got to be now! And finally, after a short series of synchronous spasms, Benjamin and Geoff wiped their hands on their shirts and parted ways.

His head thumped, and his heart pounded in his chest. The haze began to lift, adding an even more disturbing and sobering realism to events. Still, his legs gave him nothing. Face screwed up, he yanked at the lever, expecting heads to turn, but he was in the clear. He placed his hands on both rims, another swoop of the room confirming it was likely his best and only chance. A wheelchair. How difficult could it be?

"You're such a naughty boy, Terrence."

"You do have a hand in that."

His first effort was clumsy, but he finally turned the chair, pushing the right wheel and holding the left. Music played, liquor flowed, and impossibly white flesh flickered in and out of view. He swallowed hard, clenching his fists before resting his hands on the wheels.

Three.

Two.

One.

And he was off, wheeling like a madman, eyes on the door in the distance.

"Talk dirty to me, Harold."

"I think I've shit myself."

So far so good.

Simon glanced over both shoulders, relieved to see nobody chasing after him. None of what happened made any sense, but he just wanted out, never to see anyone over sixty again. Dancing and screwing like drugged-up teenagers before an apocalypse, the old fuckers put the fear of God into him.

"Choke me, George. Do it like you mean it."

Jesus fucking Christ! But he was halfway there, halfway to freedom. Laughter and squeals emerged behind him as Simon rolled the wheels like his life depended on it. Thrust. Thrust. Thrust. His fingers burned. Not a drop of saliva in his mouth. A shower—that was the first thing he'd do after calling the police. He imagined the hot water rushing over him, washing away all the badness. The leaking sores, the salty sweat from Janet's arse crack, the—

Fuuuuck!

Holding his breath, Simon watched the marble rolling across the wood. Not a marble—a glass fucking eye! Shit. Shit. Shit. Even over the music, it sounded impossibly loud, like a giant boulder smashing through all possible hopes of escape. He clenched his teeth, expecting any second for bony fingers to coil around his shoulder or for a broom to find his skull.

Nothing.

He finally afforded himself another glance over his shoulder, only to see the pasty degenerates still wrapped in their vile version of rapture. Hardly believing his luck, he set off again, his arms more responsive than ever. Only twenty feet to go, and he'd be free, the thought bringing tears to his eyes. He imagined himself wrapping his fingers around the doorknob, the rush of petrichor as he yanked the—

KNOCK. KNOCK. KNOCK.

Sure that his chest would explode, Simon watched the doorknob begin to turn. He continued his approach, arms already singing. Not another crusty. Not another crusty.

Music behind him crackled off.

Moans faded to silence.

The door shook on its hinges but remained closed. "Simon, are you in there?"

Rachel! What the fuck? He didn't turn this time, just rolled as fast as he could. Footsteps broke out behind, prompting a roar and for him to spin the wheels of fortune as quickly as possible.

"Where do you think you're going, soldier?"

Caught between a cry for help and a plea for Rachel to run to safety, his dash for freedom became frenzied and clumsy, a raised floorboard and momentum almost taking the chair over. Ten feet to go, he focussed his stare on the latch, his gateway to freedom.

"Simon, what's happening in there?" KNOCK. KNOCK. KNOCK. "I can hear things. And why is it so dark?"

No longer able to hold his tongue, Simon let out a desperate cry. "Heeeeeeeelp!"

"Simon? Simon, what's going on?"

"Call the police, Rach! Call the police and get the fuck out of here!"

"What?" KNOCK. KNOCK. KNOCK. "Simon, stop messing about and open this fucking door right now!"

And before he could let out another frustrated response, he was flying. Renewed pain surged across his skull as his cheek slammed into the ground, an immediate metallic taste at the back of his mouth. He moaned, returning his stare to the door as it rattled on its hinges. "Run," he cried, his feet scraping uselessly against the wood. "Run, Rachel!" But as someone coiled their fingers around his ankles and dragged him away, the door continued to shake.

"Tut, tut, soldier. Going AWOL is frowned upon around here."

Just before Simon disappeared around the corner, he saw Nana Ivy smoothing down her dress and approaching the door. He never felt the crack on the side of his head that finally put pay to his glasses.

Chapter Eight: Rachel's Got Moves

Beyond the old lady's shoulders, Rachel could hear whispers and shuffles. She arched her neck, catching sight of shifting silhouettes. "Simon's okay then?"

Of course he is, my dear. A lovely boy but rather cheeky. We've been having an absolute hoot."

Rachel searched the old lady's face for anything over than gummy sincerity. "It just sounded like he was in trouble. And he said something about calling the police."

"Haha. Such a joker. A likely lad, if ever I saw one." Ivy offered the warmest smile, stepping aside and ushering her in. "He's a writer, you know; had us all running around like idiots, acting out his little stories."

Rachel nodded and smiled, thinking herself silly for suspecting any different, recalling Simon's boast about winning old people over. And he was a joker, no doubt, part of his appeal not taking himself too seriously. She shut her phone and crossed the threshold into Newhaven Crescent Community Centre, the malodorous blanket instantly wrapping around her. Lord have mercy. She maintained her smile but wanted to run back outside, strip all her clothes off, and let the breeze cleanse her from the ungodly stench.

"Can I grab your coat, dear?" Ivy asked. "Sorry, what was your name again, petal?"

"It's Rachel."

"And I'm Ivy. Let me grab that coat."

"No, it's fine; thank you all the same." Rachel wondered why she felt the immediate need to be ultra-polite in front of the elderly. It was instinctive, even her posture stiffer than usual. "I won't stay long. We're going for drinks."

Nana Ivy brought her hands together and gave them a little rub. "Simon didn't say anything about a girlfriend, the dark horse."

"Oh no, it's not like that," Rachel said, running her eyes across the room. "We work together. We're—friends."

"Friends one minute, but that's where it starts." Ivy offered Rachel a wink and a sharp elbow in her side. "A couple of drinks, and he'll be playing you like a fiddle. And after a couple more, he'll be up to his nuts in yer guts."

Rachel kept smiling, but her skin offered a discomforting prickle. She turned her stare to the stage area, eye contact with the overly fond lady suddenly becoming too much. "Could you tell Simon I'm here, please?"

"Of course." Ivy slapped her hands together again. "Please excuse the mess; we're rehearsing for a little jamboree. Nothing heavy or anything. We're old and fragile, after all, but we still like a bit of a jig. Janet!"

Rachel recoiled at the sudden volume change.

"Janet!" Ivy yelled again.

She watched a burly woman emerge from the corridor. Boards under her feet vibrated as the woman approached, carrying a flustered demeanour and a smile. "And who might this lovely creature be?" she said.

"This is Simon's girlfriend," Ivy said.

"Oh, the dark horse."

"I'm not his girlfriend. We just work together."

"Friends one minute," Janet said, "But before you know it, you're up to—"

"Where is he? Simon."

Janet smiled. "He's just having a little lie-down, love. Been running around here all afternoon like a dog chasing a car. Said he was feeling a little woof."

"Woof?"

"Rough, dear, rough."

"What's your tipple," Ivy said. "We've got the lot."

Rachel looked over Janet's rounded shoulders to see others spilling into the room. No sign of Simon, though. Already regretting the decision, part of her wanted to cut her losses and run. Instead, she resignedly walked to the bar area, taking her place at one of the stools. "Whisky and coke."

"Hey, Clemmy," Ivy said. "There's fresh meat in the audience if you fancy getting on stage." The old lady poured a generous amount of whisky into a tumbler. "Got a lovely voice, she has, Rachel. Like an angel. Come on, Clementine, show her what you've got."

Rachel turned her attention to the stage. Blouse hanging open, exposing a floral bra, the white-haired lady all but leaped up the steps, doing her best to tidy her dishevelled hair before grabbing the microphone.

"Loves to perform," Janet said. "Born to do it. It's as though electricity spills from the microphone all the way down to her toes."

"There you go, my love." Ivy placed the glass before her and walked across to the gramophone. "Now, let me see." She searched through an adjacent box kicking up a spiral of dust. "Ah, here we go. This one is her absolute favourite. Gives me goose bumps when she sings it."

As the music kicked in, Rachel watched some oldies take to the dancefloor, thinking it incredibly cute and moving, even getting teary when Clementine began to sing. Her voice was indeed angelic but also filled with vulnerability, suggesting a thousand other stories beyond the words emerging. Unable to recall the last time she'd visited her grandma, there was a sudden urge to run to her house with flowers and chocolates, begging for tales of yesteryear. It was an emotional moment that took her by surprise. "Is that a gas mask?"

"Benjamin, yes," Ivy replied. "Ironically enough, he has a bit of a phobia of old people."

"Well, what do you think of our Clemmy?" Janet asked.

"She's adorable." Her opinion of Simon immediately rocketed; the thought of him risking losing his job to keep the dear old people happy, entertaining them by playing games and acting out stories to trigger imaginations buried underneath layers of life's rubble. He was certainly not her usual type, but she figured that might not be such a bad thing after the string of idiots she'd recently dated. "Really lovely."

"You look a little skinny, love," Ivy said, pulling a stool beside her. "Need a bit of fattening up. How about a slice of Nana Ivy's cherry pie? Freshly baked today."

"Oh no, it's fine. We'll probably grab something when we're out."

"Nonsense; you'll have a slice, and that's the last I'll hear of it. Nothing better than my cherry pie, is there, Janet?"

"Nothing, Ivy."

"Fresh fruit, not tinned. Anything else just gets my goat, doesn't it, Janet?"

"It does, Ivy."

"Just a slither then."

"Excellent! Janet."

"Yes, Ivy." The burly lady walked around the bar and ducked under the counter. A few seconds later, she emerged with much more than just a slither of the most wonderful-looking pie. "This will tide you over."

At Ivy's request, the room filled with more beautiful music, the old people on the dancing floor conjuring memories of old black and white movies Rachel used to watch with her grandma. It was, against all odds, becoming a wonderful end to the day. And there was an undeniable twinge of excitement at spending the evening with Simon, the joker who played make-believe to keep these folks' spirits up. Old people love me.

Rachel took another swig of her drink, nodding when Ivy offered a refill. She broke the pie's crust with her spoon, feeling immense satisfaction as she watched the magnificent red spill over into gold. "Thank you for your hospitality," she said before spooning in the first mouthful.

"Well?

"Delicious," she replied, immediately digging her spoon in again.

"Thank you, dear. Simon thought so, too."

"What's taking him so long anyway?"

"Janet will go and check on him, won't you, love?"

"Aye."

Taking another mouthful of the best-tasting pie she could recall; Rachel fondly watched the big lady head towards the corridor. A funny pair, she thought. She'd even have gone so far as to say they were adorable if it weren't for the nuts-in-guts comment. Hungry for more, she looked down at her dish, disappointed to see nearly half of it already gone.

"We do our best to keep smiling, love," Ivy said. "But it gets hard, you know. People tend to write you off when you get to a certain age."

Rachel spooned another piece of pie into her mouth. "Ageism," she concurred, bits of crust flecking the counter. "As bad as sexism." The whisky was going to her head, and she made a note to slow down. Never a good idea to turn up to a first date inebriated, not after what happened last time.

"Some don't even think of you as human, just a shell with a soul clinging on for dear life. But we feel, we grieve, we live, and we love. Laughter is key; I'll tell you that."

"A sense of humour is important," Rachel agreed between mouthfuls. "You need it in this life."

"Indeed." Ivy reached across for her hand. "If we didn't laugh, we'd cry. And company, too, solidarity in the face of adversity. If it weren't for this place, people would likely just shrivel up and die."

Guilt gnawed at Rachel's insides. She knew the scoop; the place was as good as gone. "I never want to get old, Ivy. No offence."

"None taken. And Rachel, let me ask you a question."

"Of course." She noticed a man approaching, what looked like a flower in his right hand. Suddenly feeling like the room was on a tilt, she shifted in her seat. "Ask me anything."

Ivy gave her hand a gentle squeeze. "When it came down to the crunch, when all odds were against you, what would you do to survive? How hard would you fight?"

"With everything that I bloody well had," she replied.

"I'm glad you understand."

On the release of her hand, Rachel spooned the last of the pie into her mouth. She washed it down with the dregs of whisky, an involuntary cherry-fragranced belch following that sent her into a fit of giggles. "Better out than in," Ivy said, offering a fart that had Rachel doubling over.

"Care to dance, Ma'am?"

Rachel lifted her gaze to see a man with giant ears offering a daffodil and a smile full of gums. If it weren't for this place, people would likely just shrivel up and die. She returned the smile, took the flower, and brought it to her nose. "The name's Rachel."

"No, it's Norman."

"No, my name is Rachel."

"Well, come on then, Chantelle, I haven't got all bloody day."

She offered a snort. "Rachel!"

"Stop calling me Rachel. And there's no need to shout."

The old man took her hand and escorted her towards the dance floor. She almost went down halfway across, only Norman's firm grip keeping her from hitting the deck. She laughed it off, but her legs felt strange, spongy almost. People parted before them, gracing them with broad smiles and impossibly wide eyes, one with the number one written across it. Only one old man leered in a way that made her feel uncomfortable.

"Hands off, Harry, she's mine," Norman said.

"Dibs for sloppy seconds," he replied.

As Clementine began belting out another number, Norman put an arm around Rachel's waist and brought her close. "You're very pretty, Chantelle."

Rachel laughed, deciding to let it slide. "Thank you, Norman. I think—I think you're very handsome, too."

"Huh?"

"You're very—" Her left leg gave, forcing her to squeeze her arms around Norman's waist. "Handsome."

"Ransom? What the devil are you talking about, woman?"

"Too much whisky." But she'd only had two glasses and wasn't usually a lightweight. Still, the room began to spin, its tilt more exaggerated than ever. In the background, Clementine's voice became nothing but a drawl, and wherever Rachel looked, cloudy eyes and teeth formed a kaleidoscopic nightmare of senility.

"Are you alright, love?"

Far from being alright, Rachel felt like the walls were closing in, and the floor was trying to swallow her. "Water, Norman. Think I need some—" She began to slide down her dance partner until her face pressed against his crotch.

"You're an animal, Norm."

"What's that, Harry?"

"Never-fucking mind. Hey, love, I'll let you pet my snake when you finish with the worm. Best be careful, though; it's got one hell of a bite."

Rachel's legs finally lost their fight, Norman's right loafer cushioning her fall somewhat. "My hero, Norm," she said, giggling. Clementine offered her a smile from the stage, but she was sure she could see tears running down the old lady's face. "Killing it, Clemmy. Killing it," she mumbled. Initially, Rachel thought the stage getting smaller was just another part of drinking on an empty stomach, but it soon dawned on her that someone had hold of her legs. "Where are we going?"

"To see your boyfriend."

"He's not my—"

Chapter Nine: A Work's Night In

Even with the gag in his mouth, scratching at his throat, Simon continued to scream her name. He nudged her with his feet, but she only offered an unconscious whimper.

Fuck!

Without his glasses, too, he felt even more vulnerable. Dressed in a dog costume, hands tied behind his back, legs bound, he wondered how much time they had before whatever the stiffs had planned next. Would he be forced into another round of stand-up? A spot of fetch? Naked Twister? Another sacrifice to the shadow on the wall? The sky was the fucking limit.

Fuck! Fuck! Fuck!

He was no hero, not built for this kind of stuff. The noblest thing he'd ever done was pick up an old lady after someone pushed her over and grabbed her handbag. Pushed the fucker over. He never thought of giving chase, just did the responsible thing and called the police.

Even the old lady looked at him like he was shit on her shoe. "Not everyone is Bruce Willis," he muttered to her. Better with a clipboard, for sure.

What the fuck do I do?

Being locked in a glorified cupboard with the walking dead on guard wasn't exactly a first date he could work with. Do you come here often? Yes, it smells like piss and shit, and the lighting's a bit off, but you must admit it's rather cosy. No, tap water this evening, I'm afraid, just the brown stuff from the bucket. The afternoon matinee? Yes, it's about a bunch of old people that dress people as animals and FUCKING MURDER THEM! He gritted his teeth, trying to force his hands from the yarn, but it was tighter than before and cutting into his fur. His legs were going numb, too. Contorting into a yoga-like position, he ran a paw across the wool around his ankles, identifying the tiniest knot through the material.

Rachel gave out another moan, but her eyes remained shut. Frustration setting in, Simon began pushing her with his bound feet again, his attempts getting firmer each time. Not only would this go down as the worst first date of Rachel's life, he thought, but he was also kicking the shit out of her for good measure. Finally, the poor woman's eyes began to flicker.

Simon watched through a blurry haze as realisation wrapped its stinky blanket around her, deep frown lines carving their way across her forehead as she let out a muffled cry. She began squirming against the floor, redundantly kicking out, almost catching him on the chin. Her whimpers became unbearable, something beyond fear etching across her face. With conviction, Simon moved in close and began widening his eyes and nodding as though some ancient lost code for calm-the-fuck-down. It seemed to be working, albeit slowly, her muffled pleas settling to a whimper but her eyes remaining as wide as ever.

Shuffling around on his knees, Simon beckoned her with his paws, hoping she'd understand. He glanced over his shoulder, relieved to find her responding, moving her head towards him and squinting. Initially reminding him of a film he wished he'd never seen, he urged himself to focus. Come on. Come on. After poking her in the eye, prompting a subsequent cry of protest, he finally pawed across her skin, working towards the tape. But it was useless, his furry mitts incapable of establishing any grip.

They swapped positions, Rachel managing to curl one end of the tape with a nail as she strained to look over her shoulder. After several unsuccessful and rushed attempts, she finally ripped it off, prompting a muted yelp from Simon and a series of chokes. Something was still in there. Desperate to rid his throat of the scratchiness, he leaned in again, Rachel's fingers urgently fishing out whatever it was. He took in a mouthful of air as something fell to the floor between them, any relief short-lived as he studied the large pair of crumpled men's underpants, a blurry but unmistakable yellow stain running just above the gusset.

Rachel turned, delayed shock registering in her eyes. Knowing it might be enough to send her over the edge, Simon nodded and widened his eyes three times. "It's going to be okay, Rach." He nodded some more for good measure. "I promise we will get out of this, but I need to get up close and intimate for this next bit."

Visibly shaking, Rachel nodded back, prompting Simon to bite at a tiny, exposed corner of the tape. His grunting was involuntary and inelegant, but he figured beggars couldn't be choosers. Finally, he managed to rip off the tape, subsequently using his teeth to drag the dirty undies from her mouth.

Rachel took several deep breaths, screwing her face up at the sight of the shit stain. "What the hell is this place?"

"This is Hell, Rachel. I've seen the Devil himself." In hindsight, Simon thought his words couldn't have been any less comforting: *Sorry for the trauma and all that, but I can almost guarantee things will get worse.* "But we'll get out of this, I promise." He turned around, offering his wrists. "Can you try to untie me?"

She followed suit and turned, feeling her way across the yarn to the knot. "Simon, tell me what's going on. And why the hell are you dressed as a dog?"

"These folks aren't right, Rach. We need to get out of here."

"But they seemed so sweet." She tried to work a nail under the knot, hearing it snap. "Shit! Shit. Shit! The guy with giant ears... I was dancing with him, and the next minute, I—I—"

"As I said, they ain't right. Seem sweet enough, but just like the pie, there's something bad inside."

"The pie."

"Yes, the pie. It's Ivy; she's the bad motherfucker, the leader of these crusties."

"I don't understand." Another nail snapped, moving her close to tears. "Like a cult? What do they want, Simon? Why are we here? My fucking head!"

Where to start? Where to fucking start? A series of flashbacks started rushing through his head—the lacklustre talent show, the sacrifice of the community centre pet, the subsequent orgy, and the untimely arrival of his date. "Why did you come here, Rach?"

"Trevor was losing his shit in front of everyone, wondering where you were. Made a big song and dance about getting you fired."

"That's why you came?"

"Not just that. Does it really fucking matter right now?" Yet another nail snapped, sending her into a bout of frenzied cussing and sobbing. "I can't fucking do it, Simon. Can't get any traction."

"Okay, okay. Turn around; I'll try and chew through."

"What? Oh God, Simon, what are they going to do? None of it makes any fucking sense."

Simon considered his response carefully. She was becoming hysterical, but he felt he owed her the truth. "I saw them kill Jacob. As far as I can tell, it's a sacrificial thing. One minute, it was like they were melting"—or flaking—" and the next, they were as good as new. Well, as good as old."

"What? What do you mean?"

It felt like he was narrating a story, but he'd damned sure not written anything as weird, figuring a tale of this ilk more suited to those with padded cells, talking to people who weren't there. "It was like a strange healing ritual, somehow freezing the ageing process and staving off death. Everyone was chanting in tongue and getting over-excited. And then I saw the Devil's shadow on the wall, watched as it approached and fed on Jacob's soul." He took a breath, watching Rachel trying to process his words. That should do it, he thought; if she were not beside herself before, she would be now. "But it's going to be okay, Rach," he added, hearing the uncertainty in his voice. "It's going to be okay."

Rachel's continued stunned silence prompted him to get to work on the yarn. He dug his teeth in and began to pull, a series of discomforting vibrations running through his jaw and neck. He had a thing about teeth, unable to remember the last time he visited the dentist. He suddenly wondered if he'd ever see one again.

"Jacob?" Rachel finally said. "Jacob from work? But he's been gone—"

"Months." He remembered the note shoved under the door. "Was dressed as a dog when I saw him, just like I am now. Even had a convincing bark. He looked terrible, Rachel. God only knows what he went through."

"Well, that's not fucking terrifying." Rachel began to shake even more vigorously, even her lips untouched by the urgency running through her. "Can we please get out of here, Simon? Please!"

He went back to chewing. Rats. Big fuckers, too. Progress was slow, but he managed to work through some of the fibres, encouraged by Rachel's perfume that helped counter the stench that had set up home in his nostrils.

"What did they do to him? Jacob?"

Make your fucking mind up, love; do you want me to talk or chew? Still, grateful to rest his aching jaw, Simon took a breath. "The same thing they probably did to those other missing folks around town," he replied, trying to skip the question. "But who would suspect a bunch of stiffs?"

"Oh shit. It's all coming back to me."

"Please keep still while I chew. It hurts my teeth."

"Ivy—she asked me what I'd do to survive. How hard I'd fight. I said I'd do everything."

"Please."

"'I'm glad you understand,' she said. Oh, God. Oh, Jesus. Oh—"

"Keep fucking still!"

Rachel's posture stiffened, allowing him to get back to work. Practiced technique paying dividends, Simon worked through the yarn with a new-found efficiency. His teeth sang, but the frayed fibres encouraged him. Come on. Come on! Finally, Rachel yanked herself free, the wool falling to the floor. Fuck, yeah! With renewed optimism, he watched her lean over and quickly work at the threads around her ankles, luck playing its part in a slightly looser knot.

"Me, me, me, me," Simon muttered as she cast the yarn aside. He turned and offered his paws hopefully, already mulling over the next stage of the plan. Or at least trying to come up with one. He knew the door was locked, but considered there might be a way of opening it from the inside. "Hurry up, Rach. We have to get out of here."

"Captain fucking obvious." Teeth gritted, she worked at the yarn, struggling to get leverage, her nails bending back.

"Don't worry about your nails; just get me the fuck out."

"I'm not worried about my fucking nails, Simon! The knots are too tight."

"Chew then!"

"What?"

"I chewed for you!"

After another failed attempt and broken nail, Rachel finally got to biting at the wool. Unable to imagine any great relationship ever started from chewing, she knew this would be their first and final date. "I can't do it; it hurts my teeth."

Before any further argument, squeaking floorboards drew their attention to the door. Sure her heart would explode, Rachel grabbed Simon's front right leg, "What do we do?" But he had nothing for her, his stomach churning with dread.

Fuck. Fuck. Fuck. "You have to make a run for it, Rach."

"What?"

"We might not get another chance. There's a latch on the front—"

"I can't, Simon. I can't."

"You have to, Rach. Go and get help."

The shuffling got louder. He imagined Janet twirling the broom.

"Simon, I—"

"Help me up. Push me in front of the door."

"What? Oh, Christ." She hooked her arms under his shoulders and helped guide him towards the door. "I can't. I can't."

"Do or die, Rachel." Simon shook his head aggressively, trying to snap into the moment, the giant ears flapping on either side not helping. "As soon as it opens, you push me as hard as you can and run."

"I don't want to die."

"Then make it!"

After several incoherent yells, the footsteps started again.

Breath held, they waited.

A key rattled in the lock. The doorknob turned.

Simon readied himself, hoping Rachel had it in her. Hoping he did.

"Is everyone ready?" the voice boomed, confirming it was Janet on the other side of the door. "A busy night, huh?" she said, yanking the door open.

Broom in hand, Janet's jaw dropped. "What the—" Before she could react, Simon was thrust towards her, offering a growl. He managed to clamp his teeth into her saggy neck, a salty metallic taste forming at the back of his throat. Even as Janet thrust the broom into his chest, he refused to let go, taking her blows. "Get her!" the big lady screamed.

Like a dog with a bone, Simon continued chewing on her flesh as she manically swung herself around. He heard distant cries and, from the corner of his eye, saw Rachel halfway to the door. Other crusties had started to scramble after her but were in no danger of breaking any world records. She's going to make it. She's going to fucking make it!

Janet offered a grunt, sensing advantage was swinging back her way. She even smiled as she finally freed his jaws from her neck. "Naughty doggy." Teeth gritted, she manically ripped at his fur, finally getting a decent grip and hurling him towards the wall with herculean strength.

Simon's head buried into plasterboard, but it didn't stop him from taking satisfaction in the bleary streams of red flowing over the ripples in her neck. He offered a sharp bark. "Fuck you, you psychotic piece of rotting flesh." Just in time to see Rachel work the latch and swing the door open, he turned, a smile working across his face.

Freedom!

Ending thoughts of how good the rush of fresh air must have felt, the broom found his skull again.

Chapter Ten: Smoking Kills

Relief brought tears as Rachel stumbled into the car park, squinting into the late afternoon sun. She tried to clear her head and straighten her story, but it all seemed too far-fetched to be true. She could almost imagine the police officers' faces as she recounted tales of pie, dog costumes, and a cult of sacrificial old codgers.

"Rachel!"

She blinked away the floaters. "Trevor? Trevor, thank Christ!" The sight of his familiar face was too much. She went to the ground and began to sob. "They've got Simon, Trevor! You have to help!"

"It's okay, Rachel. It's okay." He made his way over, resting a hand on the base of her neck, the usual cancer stick hanging from the corner of his mouth. "Breathe. Just breathe."

Taking in mouthfuls of air, she reached for Trevor's age-spotted hand and pulled herself up. "The old people, Trevor. They're not right, not normal. They killed Jacob, and they—they—"

"Slow down, Rach. Slow down," he snapped his head left and right, offering a puff of smoke. "We'll sort this mess out."

"Please, Trevor. We have to get out of here. We have to—"

"Shh, Rachel. No need to be scared; everything will be okay."

She couldn't stop herself from shaking, words running into each other in her head. "We need to call the police. We need to—"

"What? What do we need to do, Rachel?"

The man looked far too calm. Far too unruffled. Dread prickled its way across her skin and began tunnelling into her chest. She stepped back, grateful that her legs supported her. "What are you doing here?"

He took a final drag on the cigarette, flicked it to the ground, and offered a shrug. "If you want a job done properly."

Rachel took another step back, her heart thrumming towards a dangerous crescendo. In a gesture of futile defence, she held a hand out towards him.

"What is it, Rach?"

Clarity had finally arrived, but it had brought more than she had bargained for. "Your cancer last year... at death's door one minute, and the next, as good as new." As good as old.

"Beat the odds, for sure." Trevor took a step forward. "More than one way to skin a dog."

Swallowing hard, clenching her fists, Rachel prepared herself to run. Do or die, Rachel. But her legs suddenly felt leaden, that same feeling of sinking into the ground.

"Sometimes, it's all about who you know," Trevor continued, giving his chest a Tarzan-like thump. "When you're old, you'll understand, Rach. It's nothing personal, just survival."

"No. No. Please, Trevor, just—" Any further pleas were stifled as a big arm looped around her neck, the window for escape now over.

"You should have just left that streak of piss alone, Rach."

Rachel's scream remained trapped as the giant hand clamped around her mouth. "It will all be over soon, love," Janet said, dragging her back towards the darkness. Trevor followed, sliding another ciga-rette from his pocket. "It's a good job that I turned up when I did. We really can't be this sloppy moving forward, Janet."

"Agreed. But we didn't expect another visitor." She glanced over her shoulder, making sure the path was clear. "Will this stall them, do you think?"

"They can't do anything without the paperwork." Placing the ciga-rette between his lips, Trevor offered a silent fuck you to all the doctors who told him he should quit. "And rumour has it a possible new location has appeared out of the woodwork."

"Oh, I wish we didn't have this hanging over our heads, Trev."

"You and me both; I'm more than bloody ready for retirement." He offered her a smile. "But I think the odds are swinging in our favour, Janet. All these folks going missing; this place is going to the dogs. What about the cars?"

"I'll get Albert to move them after he's finished with the bodies. I'm so glad you're here; that one-eyed fucker makes a shit Martini."

After smoothing his photograph back on the wall, Trevor took position behind the bar, much to everyone's delight. "Sorry I missed the first one, gang," he said, "but let's make this encore a belter." The crusties offered their approval and continued setting up the room.

Figuring his quota done for quite some time, Trevor nodded to-wards Ivy, who returned it with her warm smile. He lit his cigarette and started organising the playlist for the evening.

Chapter Eleven: A Dog's Life

Simon snapped his eyes open, the subsequent pain intense and immediate. If he ever got hold of that fucking broom, he thought, he'd drive it so far up Janet's arse that it would tickle her tonsils.

Were the police already on their way, he wondered?

Music spilled under the door, a familiar tune, but he wasn't in the mood for a pop quiz. He could hear distant voices, too, and could feel the floor vibrating beneath him. The crazy fuckers are it again; one last shindig before the shit goes down. He felt sorry for them initially, losing their precious centre, all pity going out the window as soon as he realised Newhaven Crescent Community Centre's stage was a glorified altar, a pissy place of sacrifice. He wondered how many people they had offered, relieved he wouldn't be one of them.

That first taste of fresh air. A nice hot shower. Two small steps, but a giant leap for a man in a dog costume with a head full of saggy balls and breasts. Such thoughts of freedom caused his skin to prickle.

"Come on, Rach."

He rolled over to his side, trying to get into a more comfortable position, exposing the tear in the suit and the note sticking from his gaping pocket. Evidence. *The crusty old fuckers are going downtown.* After several unsuccessful attempts, he finally managed to grip the piece of paper, urgently flattening it down and arching his neck to reduce the fuzziness. It was still barely legible, scribbled as though written with a—paw. He arched his neck, trying to bring it into focus.

Help!

Whoever is reading this, run for your life. Call the police. These people are twisted.

My name is Jacob Scott. I have a wife and two children who will be missing me.

They drugged me, put me in a dog costume, and locked me in this cupboard. All they ever feed me is kibble and cherry pie.

The big woman—Janet—sometimes lets me out, but only on a leash and never outside the centre. She throws a stick and commands me to fetch it. If I refuse, she hits me with a broom. I'm not allowed to talk, only to bark. And sometimes, when they have one of their jamborees, they make me do other stuff too. Stuff I don't care to talk about.

I don't know how long I've been here, but I think they plan to kill me soon... the way they look at me these days. I've been throwing up recently and messing myself. I don't feel well, quite ~~woof~~ rough of late.

"Poor fucker," Simon said, the thought of the man's trauma tightening the skin around his skull. "Not me, Jay. Jacob. Help is on the way."

I tried to escape once, but they caught and beat me. Thought I was going to die. The leader—Ivy—said as long as I did as I was told, she would spare me. But I've heard them whispering. And something else that I'll sound crazy for mentioning, but hey, I'm dressed in a dog costume and bark on command... I've seen a shadow on the wall, watching, waiting. It has claws and horns as if—

Hell, these folks scare me to death.

I've listed the names of the evil fuckers below. I hope they burn in hell!

Liz (puppet)

Harry (persistent masturbator)

Albert (one eye)

Geoff (two eyes, but all over the fucking place)

Jimmy (foot like a boomerang)

Maud (no bowel control)

Benjamin (gas mask)

Trevor (my employer)

Norman (ears)

...

Simon felt the blood rushing from his face. Trevor (my employer). It didn't even register on the first read. "That fuck." His body stiffened with rage; his teeth ground together, causing his jaw to ache. He read it over and over to make sure his disadvantaged eyes weren't somehow playing tricks. "That fucking fuck!" He started to imagine all the different ways he could bring pain to the old bastard, how loud he could make the arsehole scream. "It's game over, Trevor. Once I'm out of here, you are fucking done, mate. I'll SHUT THIS FUCKING PLACE DOWN, SO HELP ME!"

Thoughts turned back to Rachel. She'd probably be crying, reliving the trauma as an officer tried to calm her down. Poor woman, what a thing to have gone through. He wanted to be there for her now, reassuring her that everything would be okay. The thought wouldn't escape him that perhaps trauma might even bring them together, bonding them in a way nobody else could possibly understand. It would be a slow process, but through mutual understanding, they could emerge better than ever, strong enough to take on the world. They could get married, have kids... grow old together.

"You're fucking delusional, Simon."

He let his back fall against the wall, thoughts again turning to a nice shower and a big juicy steak with all the trimmings. Perhaps a nice glass of red instead of a pint. The idea made him giddy, the first step in distancing himself from the events he'd experienced. What then? Therapy? He thought that even trained professionals would surely cower from bearing witness to such debauchery. Trying to spin a positive, he swore he'd never take his youth for granted again.

As floorboards creaked, he backed up against the storeroom wall, heart rate on the up. Too early for it to be the cops, he wondered who it was, hoping to high hell it wasn't Janet, broom in hand, ready for revenge. More laughter and excited cries made it under the door as the footsteps got louder still. And that song playing through that godawful gramophone; he recognised it but couldn't for the hell of him conjure up the name.

The door clicked. The knob began to turn.

Not Janet, please. And not Ivy. Anyone but—

He didn't trust his eyes at first. "Trevor?"

The man smiled, placing a silver bowl on the floor. "Brought you some water; thought you might be thirsty."

Simon felt a growl in his throat. His body began to spasm as if making up for its previous redundancy. "You're done, Trevor. You're fucking done. Rachel's calling you in as we speak. They'll arrest your saggy arses and shut this fucking place down."

"Rachel?" Trevor offered an evil laugh that would have given even the toughest bond villains a run for their money. "Rachel's in hair and makeup. The girls are having a hoot getting her ready for the second act."

"No! No-no-no. That's not—there's no fucking way." But the man standing before Simon showed no signs of bluffing. "She was out. She was—"

"Janet will be over soon for puppy training. She's old school, if you know what I mean, but gets the job done. My preference was Rachel, but the rest seem to love you."

Old people love me. Old people love me. "But she was out."

"Three double scotches, barman," someone shouted over the music.

"Be over in a second, Mavis," he replied, not taking his eyes off Simon. "Just introducing myself to the new pet."

"I'll fucking kill you, Trevor." Simon lunged forward but ended up face down near the pissy bucket. Couldn't write this stuff. Couldn't dream it up. "I'll rip your fucking head off and shit down your neck. I'll tear the skin off your fucking face."

"The sooner Janet starts her obedience classes, the better." Trevor offered another leery smile as he nudged the silver bowl with his foot. "I'll be back with some kibble later." With that, he slammed the door shut behind him.

Click.

Plunged into darkness, albeit even blacker than before, Simon rested his head against the wall. "She was out. She was out." And as he contemplated the hopelessness of it all, the song's name finally found its way into his head.

Witchcraft.

The end

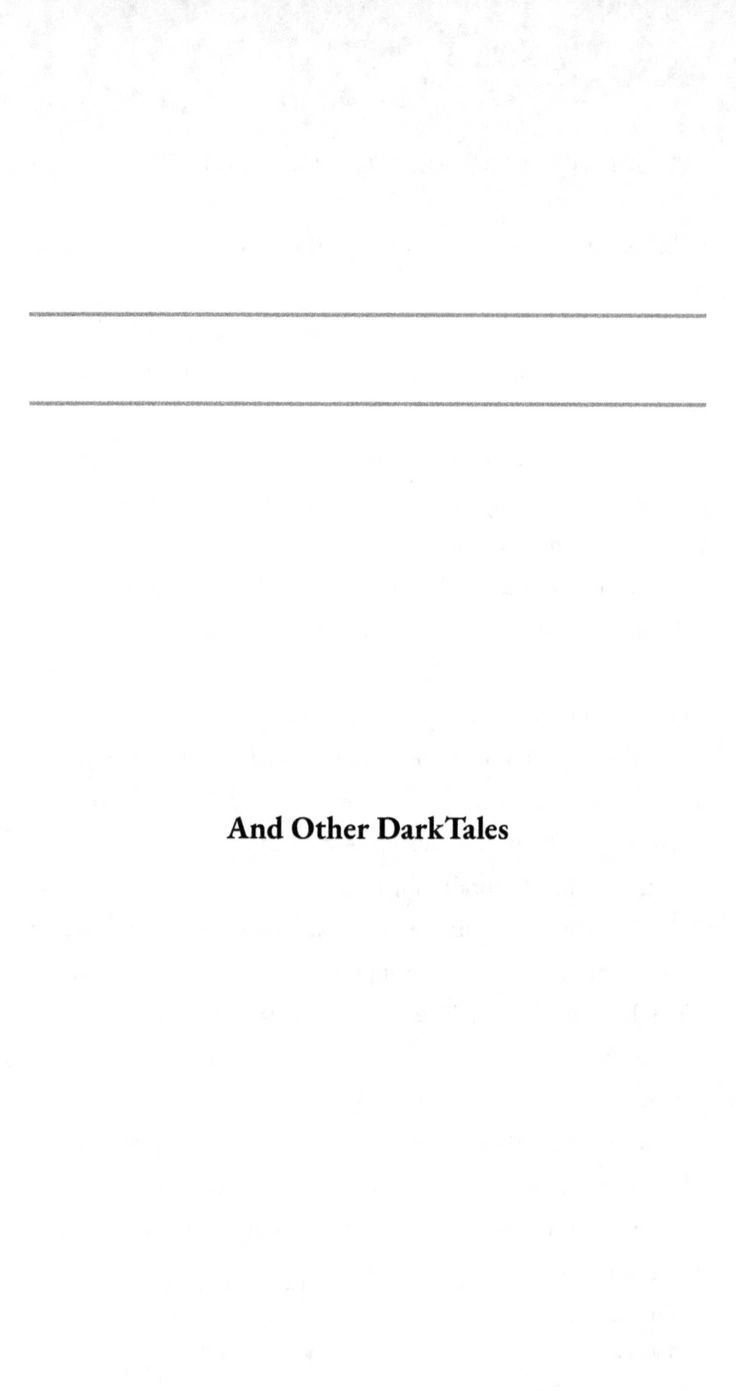

And Other Dark Tales

You Only Live Once

Gerald's already half-cut, sniffing around her again, doused in that aftershave that smells like a used towel. The man has no boundaries—at a friend's funeral of all places.

God bless you, Bernie.

The cheesy bastards even brought out the brogues and trilby for tonight, and as for that blinding yellow shirt, Jesus wept. He performs a little tap-dance, well, three taps and a wince, an embarrassing display like something from a geriatric wildlife documentary.

"Please allow me the pleasure of providing you with further lubrication, young Els," he says, breaking out into that god-awful gummy smile. He puffs out his sparrow chest and pulls out the stool next to her, adjusting his hat on the way down as if he's Paul bloody Newman.

"Oh, I think I've had enough, Gerald," she says, too classy to tell him where to go. "If I have any more, one of you lot will be carrying me home."

"I say, barman. Two more whiskies, please; easy on the ice." He flashes his guns, more like pocket pistols. "I've got you covered, Els."

"Maybe just a tipple then."

"That's the way. You only live once," he says, sliding his skinny little ass even closer to her. "Ask Bernie."

She averts her gaze towards the piano, biting at her lip. "Could do with a bit of music, though; the place is like a wake."

"Allow me," I say, noting her glistening eyes.

"Speak of the bloody dead," Gerald mutters.

"Any requests, Elsie?"

"Got one for you, Eric; how about you just fuck off and die?" Gerald says. "Should have been you before him."

"Elsie?" I take my place at the piano, lifting the fallboard. "What do you reckon?"

She forces a smile. "How about Sweet Caroline? It was Bernie's favourite."

"It was indeed." With a grimace, I stretch out my fingers and begin to play, feeling Gerald's eyes burning into the back of my head and enjoying every minute of it. He's only five years younger at seventy-two, but the way he carries on, you'd think he was Dustin fucking Bieber, or whatever they call that pesky kid with skin like a baby's bum and stupid fucking haircut. I glance over my shoulder and flash Elsie a smile. She smiles back and even begins to mouth the words, her watery eyes outsparkling the glitter on her gown. Soon, others begin leaving the finger-platter to gather round, finding their voices between mouthfuls of liquor and cocktail sausage.

"We love you, Bernie," someone shouts from the back of the group.

The crusty crowd place their drinks on the tables and join hands, reciting the song word for word, lyrics imprinted on otherwise amnesic minds. I feel the boards beneath my feet vibrating, spirals of dust launching into the air as they stomp their feet in time to the music. Not Gerald, though; his brogues are as still as can be, and arms folded, he's sulking like a school bully who's been given a wedgie by the new kid.

The volume intensifies to a proper old-school knees-up, and it brings a lump to my throat, bittersweet melancholy at all the lock-ins, laughs, and drama. I imagine Bernie in the group's centre, his rosy cheeks, his warm and infectious smile, the loudest of them all. I can hear his voice in my head, hitting every note. I can see him standing there, tapping his fingers against his rotundness, bringing his colossal feet down onto the wooden floor. I loved that man like a brother.

After umpteen repeat verses, the song finally begins drawing to a close with several pleas for me to play it over. But the streaks of mascara running down Elsie's face have me urgently rattling off the last few chords, especially as I note the old snake, Gerald, slithering towards her.

"He wouldn't have wanted tears, Els," I hear Gerald say.

Too late.

"Here, sit down, my love," he says in a voice that makes me cringe.

"Take my handkerchief, Els," I say, finally making it to the bar and hovering a hand over her shoulder.

"She's fine," Gerald says, wafting his bony hand at me. "What did you have to go and play that song for anyway? Look at the state of her."

"It was lovely, Eric," Elsie says, taking my handkerchief and dabbing at the corner of her eyes. "A really fitting tribute to a wonderful man."

Gerald shuffles around, trying to block me with his flat bottom and bony elbows. "Give the lady some space."

The guy's a handful at the best of times, but tonight he's really getting my goat.

"Barman," he says, another round.

"I'm fine, Gerald." She offers a sniffle. "No more for me. It's all a bit too emotional."

"Nonsense! A couple more, and then I'll walk you home. You can play me that Frankie Valli record you were talking about."

"I'm quite sure, Gerald. Thank you," Elsie says, still all class, all regal-like.

"The lady said she's had enough," I say, my voice as firm as I can make it.

"Come on, Els; don't listen to that wrinkly old bastard. Just one more for the road."

I give him a prod on the back. "Leave her be, Gerald."

He offers me another waft of his hand. "Push off, pipsqueak."

Pipsqueak? An archaic term I've not heard for decades. But somehow, it works, getting under my leathery skin, making my old blood boil. Regretting it almost immediately, I give him a firmer prod on the shoulder, wincing as the feedback rides through my bones.

He turns, lips curled over his teeth.

"She's obviously upset, Gerald. Perhaps just leave her be, eh?"

"Mind your fucking business."

The crowd turns. Silence.

"She's a friend," I say, feeling eyes on me from all directions. "She is my business."

He shuffles up to me, our noses less than an inch apart, offering a view of every errant hair in his cavern-like nostrils. "Jesus Christ, what have you been eating?" I say, hardly believing the words are mine. This isn't me, you see. I'm not brave.

"Pickled eggs," he replies. "Taste just like your missus used to."

I hear Elsie's sharp intake of breath and oohs and aahs from the crowd. Unable to find a suitable comeback, I'm shaking, mouth opening and closing. He knows he's likely blown it with Elsie but doesn't seem to care, his focus on me now, and there's a look in his eye I've never seen before. Am I expected to hit him? I'm seventy-seven. My arm would likely turn to dust.

He moves in closer still, pushing his forehead into mine. "Margie was always too good for you."

I've never been a fighter. Hard to believe, but even at my ripe old age, I've never had a proper scrap in my life. Even when I found out about the affair, I drove to the ocean instead of confronting anyone. Screamed at the waves until my voice ran hoarse. Several hours later, I returned home, kissed my wife on the forehead, and made dinner as though nothing had happened. I rubbed her feet that night, three hours straight, and then cried myself to sleep. They stopped seeing each other not long after that, but it wasn't at my hands.

Skull against skull, he forces me back a step. "She said you were boring. Too predictable."

Thoughts of confrontation send my stomach spinning, always have. Fight or flight, and I'm already checking in my luggage. Blood pounds in my ears, and my heart feels like it might explode—all the feelings of adrenaline but without the balls to back it up.

"No spark. No passion or excitement. A lapdog, she said, always getting under her feet. Sucked the life right out of her."

The crowd has noticed, beginning to gather around, the room alive with expectation. I look to the barman, but he appears exclusively apathetic, his attention drawn towards the small TV.

"I turned her back on, though; made her light up like a fucking Christmas tree."

My arm twitches, but the thought of lifting it, curling my fingers into a fist, and swinging makes my skin tighten. Behind his shoulder, I see Elsie looking at me, eyes wide, lips forming a circle as though she's trying to whistle.

"Never mind her. She wouldn't be interested in a limp dick like you."

It's a better insult, no doubt, but more of a blanket statement for all the males in the room. He drives me back against the piano, the fallboard coming down hard, creating a Laurel and Hardy sound effect. I want to run. I want to hide. Another fine mess. "This has been a long time coming," he says, grabbing my shirt collar with his left hand and pulling back his right arm, ready to unleash.

"Wait," someone from the crowd says.

Lionel! It's Lionel! My little orange knight in shining armour. "What about a challenge?" he squeaks, arriving at our shoulders, all smiles and fake tan, a natural showman.

"Step back, Oompa-Loompa," Gerald says. "I'm going to knock his bloody block off."

I squeeze my eyes shut, leaning back as far as possible, grimacing for pain. I've never hated anyone so much, anger flowing through me, drowning me from the inside. If only I could pull the plug and let it out. Christ, it's not like I have anything to live for, anything to lose. But fear has always ruled my life, stopped me from chasing my dreams, and led me to not even a mediocre existence. He's right; she was too good for me. Even my reflection in the bathroom mirror tells me so.

"Look; it's fairly obvious Eric isn't up for a fight," the little man says, squeezing between us, creating a sandwich of crusty white with a cheddar filling, "but in a bid to finally settle all your differences, what about a challenge of sorts? You'd be up for that, Eric, yeah?"

I open my eyes and nod, unsure of what I'm letting myself in for. "I guess."

Gritting his teeth and lips curling to a snarl, Gerald pulls his arm back another inch. His breathing is quick and erratic, an occasional croak escaping his throat. "Pathetic," he says, and I can't help but recoil as he makes to punch me but instead releases my shirt and steps back.

"And at the end of it, no more of this," Lionel says. "No gloating, no more handbags at dusk. Hatched will be buried. Done and dusted. How about it?"

Gerald shrugs, his eyes still burning into mine. I shrug back.

"It's settled then," Lionel says, patting us both on our shoulders and heading off towards the exit. "I've got an idea for the first one."

There's a buzz of excitement at the opening of the double doors, people shuffling out, the cool air rushing in, a sobering breeze dissipating some of the ethanol molecules.

"Can't we just sing Sweet Caroline again?" I shout after them. But this crowd is suddenly hungry for something else. I saw it in his eyes, too; resentment at its most pure, aged and matured for decades in a semi-stable environment but about to be uncorked. This isn't going to end well; I can feel it.

"Old people are fucking nuts," I hear the barman say as I make my way to the doors.

"You could have stepped in," I mumble on my way out.

Without turning his gaze from the small TV, he flicks me the bird.

Ahead, even Elsie looks excitable, a spring in her step as she's carried with the crowd, likely the thought of two men competing over her, feeding snippets of old black and white matinees. I thought perhaps she would step in, insist we both begin acting like adults, but she turns and smiles, waving a bony fist in the air like a commander spurring on her battalion.

"Elsie!" I say, but my laughter is swallowed by the volume of the crowd, the audience for whatever shenanigans our orange host has in store. Too late to back out anyway. I've already shamed myself by not putting up my dukes, and it's pension day tomorrow. I'll be a bloody laughingstock.

The chill penetrates the last of my whisky shield as I step outside, an involuntary shudder running along my curved spine. The large full moon looks down on me unempathetically and only seems to fuel the animalistic nature of the audience, all eyes, gums, and teeth. Gerald snaps his head towards me, giving me the thumbs down.

I'm beginning to envy my dear friend, Bernie. What the hell would he make of all this? I imagine him looking down on us from heaven, a pint of Guinness in one hand and a pork pie in the other, his iron wool-like beard collecting what falls from this mouth. Christ, who am I kidding? He'd be rolling on the floor in bloody stitches.

God bless your soul, Bernie.

"Gather round, folks, gather round," Lionel says, rubbing his hands together, neon light spilling from the twenty-four-hour superstore further illuminating his excited face. I watch them swarm around him, a fraternity of thirty or so elderlies with well over two thousand years of life experience between them. They bustle and whisper, preparing to watch two old frats or two old farts, more precisely, take part in a liquor-induced suburban version of the Senior Olympics. "It seems we have an old-fashioned duel on our hands," he says. "Two gentlemen, competing for the hand of our lovely Elsie. Els, what say you? The best out of three. Are you of acceptance that the winner will have the pleasure of your company for dinner?"

Please say no. Put an end to this nonsense.

She blushes, offering a little snigger. "Well, I have been wanting to use those coupons for that little Italian joint on Pakington Street."

So, there it is. My last chance to escape this fiasco has just been snapped away by someone I labelled as royalty only a few minutes ago.

I turned a blind eye to how quickly she put away those jellied eels, but this is even harder to swallow, if you pardon the pun.

"You best book that table under the name Gerald," my adversary says, giving his knuckles a crack.

"What's the first challenge, Lionel?" someone says; Arthur, I think it was. He's only got one leg. Why can't I be facing off against him?

Our host begins snapping his head left and right, breath peppering the air, eyes almost spinning with excitement. "I'm thinking."

"Come on, Lionel' it's freezing out here." Another voice from the crowd. Patricia, I think. Hair like candy floss and a penchant for toffees and farting in enclosed spaces.

"I've got it!" With his finger in the air, Lionel cuts a path through the group to the side of the road.

Others begin to gather, too: Youngsters, middle-aged folk, the kind you'd be more likely to associate with such a ridiculous display. Between pubs, most likely, bemused and full of inebriated smiles, they watch on as the little tanned man makes his way back to the centre of the group, slaking the only slightly more orange traffic cone behind him. "What the hell is this happy horseshit?" one of them says.

"Alright," Lionel says, dropping the cone and clapping his hands together. "First event is a throwing challenge. From this lamp post here, furthest throw wins."

Gerald steps forward. "Piece of piss." He circles his arms as he makes his way towards Lionel, the crowd offering murmurs of encouragement. "Hold this for me," he says to Elsie, offering the hat.

"When you're ready, Gerald," Lionel says.

He slides a couple of fingers inside the top of the cone and clamps his thumb on the side. "Reminds me of your missus again, Eric." The crowd watches with bated breath as he begins a pendulum-like motion, his face a picture of concentration, his waist-high pants rising and falling, occasionally revealing grey socks and pasty shins.

"Get on with it then," someone from the younger section of the crowd yells. "The suspense is killing me."

And with a roar, Gerald finally releases the cone. Face red, veins in his saggy neck, purple and popping, he steps back and snaps his head towards Lionel. "It slipped! It fucking slipped." His eyes are wide and wild as he marches towards the little man. "That doesn't count. We get three tries, yeah?"

"Only one. Referee's decision is final."

Gerald snatches his hat from Elsie and sinks into the wrinkly crowd. "Fucking satsuma on legs."

"Measured from the lamp post to its nearest point, please," Lionel says, unperturbed and professional. "Eric, take your place."

I rotate my arms but hear something pop on the third revolution and decide not to push my luck. The cone doesn't look far away, seven or eight feet perhaps. I might be able to do this. What's my play here? Pendulum method, two hands, swing from the side? Christ, what am I doing with my life?

"Six and a half strides," Linda says, a hand at the base of her spine as she hobbles back to the pavement, dragging the cone behind her.

I didn't anticipate it being so heavy, my fingers biting with arthritis as I slake the cone towards me. Okay, here goes nothing. One swing, but give it everything: that's the plan. Inhale. Exhale. Inhale. All eyes are on me. My stomach churns. Fight or flight, and once again, I'm looking through the airplane window, holding onto my one-way tick-et. I lift the cone, bring it behind me, and—fuuuuuuuuccccccck!

Laughter explodes all around, but it's Gerald's pink gums that pop out from the crowd. I can hear his guffaw in my head, can see the younger him screwing my wife, an image that's played out countless times and has never faded. "You're supposed to throw it in front of you, you silly old bastard," he says, stepping forward with a fist in the air. "Chalk one up for me, Lionel."

Fucking fucking fingers! I curl them into a fist, wincing in agony as my knuckles turn white. I'm trembling violently, blood whooshing in my ears, watching as Gerald gives some of the crowd a high-five. The cocky fucker even performs a spin, grabbing at his crotch and lifting his trilby high in the air. Christ, I hate that man!

To my left, Elsie offers me a look of pity. To my right, the younger crowd disperses, deciding they've seen enough and wanting their last beer, likely needing a chaser now. "I hope I never live that long," one of them says.

"What's next, Lionel?" someone says.

"Let me think."

"What about an arm-wrestle? Inside where it's warm, and there's ale."

"No, no, no. We've had strength already." Lionel, the games master, strokes his chin. You can almost hear the marble rattling around. "Wait!" Raising a stubby little finger in the air again, he makes his way into the middle of the road, beckoning us to follow. "Glasses off, gents. Line up next to me if you will."

We do as we're told, falling in line on either side of our fluorescent friend. I don't even try and guess what's going on in his demented little mind. Gerald glances towards me, giving me a look as though I'm shit on his shoe. If only I had the stomach and the strength to take the fucker down.

"That blue Ford over there, gents. Whoever gets the number plate correct or closest to, wins the next challenge."

"You've got to be fucking kidding," someone from the remaining right section of the crowd hollers. "And I thought snooker was boring." He walks into the night, shaking his head, the others following or veering off in a different direction.

It's just the 'farternity' again now.

"Gerald, as the winner of the last challenge, you go first."

"Fucking ridiculous. I can't even see a blue fucking Ford." He sticks his wrinkly neck out and crumples his face like a paper bag. "I'm serious. Where the fuck is it?"

"Are you conceding this one then, Gerald?"

"Stupid bloody games!"

"You weren't saying that when we were throwing traffic cones around," I say.

"Shut it, pipsqueak," he says, old schooling it with the insult again.

"A deal is a deal," Lionel says. "Referee's decision is final."

"Fuck's sake." He throws his hands in the air and disappears into the crowd. "A fix is what it is!"

I squint into the night, the neon lights and the water on the road creating a distorted, blurry scene of colour. But it makes no odds. That blue Ford belongs to a butcher called Fred, who lives two doors down from me. I could recite his plate in my sleep. Not wanting to invite the risk of foul play, I make a shot of it. "B... U... 4... C... and is that an H?" Things are looking up; fifty percent off my pork chops and now this.

"He's almost right," Arthur shouts from further down the street. "But it's a five, not a four."

"We have a winner, folks. That means," Lionel says, drumming his bony fingers against his chest, "it's time for a decider. The main event."

"What's it going to be, Lionel?" someone asks. "A fucking hearing test or a coughing competition?"

Mocking sniggers spread like wildfire, and Lionel's face soon ignites, too. He's losing the crowd and knows he needs something special for the finale. "A race!" he cries, picking up the cone. "A good old-fashioned forty-yard dash."

Gerald and I exchange a look as we follow Lionel towards the soccer field, our faces giving nothing away. I can't remember the last time I ran. It could have been the late nineties. The crowd's buzz is back as they chatter between themselves, asserting their favourites for the 10.20 at ole knacker's yard. If we were horses, someone would be waiting at the finishing line with a shotgun.

It's damp, slippery, and so bloody dark as we reach the field. Even the walk across has set my arthritis off. Shoulder to shoulder, Gerald and I watch Arnold striding out towards the centre of the field.

"Once a loser, always a loser," Gerald says.

"Look, Gerald. This is silly. We'll both likely cause ourselves an injury, and this is supposed to be Bernie's wake, for Christ's sake. I really don't—"

"I could have made her so happy," he says. "It was pity, you know, that's all. She felt sorry for you, like a puppy with three legs."

"Okay, gents, take your places. The goal line is the finishing post. Els, you give the countdown."

"It's so exciting," she says, joining Lionel at the cone, my opinion of her dropping rapidly.

We follow suit to encouragement from the crowd, "Break a leg" and "Don't die" are a couple of the more memorable chants. I observe the crowd on the finish line; forty yards suddenly seems a hell of a long way. My stomach knots, and my heart pounds.

Lionel nods. "When you're ready, Els."

"May the best man win," she says. "Three."

I'm seventy-seven years old.

"Two."

Three hip replacements; work that fucker out.

"One."

I should be in bed with a mug of cocoa and Gardener's Weekly.

"Go!"

The crowd explodes as we lumber from the starting line. Every move is agony, but I know the pain will likely be tenfold tomorrow. I hear Gerald's rattle next to me as I focus on the goalposts ahead, my head beginning to spin, my skin tightening around my skull. The ground is thankfully soft, but still, each impact rides up my bones.

I can't see him, though. I'm winning. Somehow, I'm winning!

I grit my teeth and stagger onwards, only momentum keeping me from going face down. As my left foot slides from beneath me, I almost tumble, but I'm still up; no sign of my younger competitor. The crowd cheers, fists in the air, and a couple of walking sticks, too. I see Elsie's face, eyes shining through the darkness, guiding me in like a tractor beam. I'm doing it. I'm—

Shit!

I hit the ground like the sack of bones I am, pain exploding through every part of me, the taste of blood and grass in my mouth, and my underpants riding high. Winded and helpless, I can only watch as Gerald staggers his way towards the finish to encouragement from an audience who so quickly strayed to the other side. He raises both hands in a victory gesture as he approaches the line.

And just like that, the games are over.

The fair(ish) maiden has her victor.

Gerald turns, all teeth. He even has the audacity to jump up and grab the goal's crossbar, hanging like a chimp on its last legs—one last show of strength. I don't know what it is, the sight of his chimp-like gums, the pitiful stares of the crowd, or the full moon's pull, but I force myself to my feet even though my limbs scream at me to stay down.

Nerve endings sing, my muscles pop, and the vein in my head pounds its beat.

Three.

Two.

One.

Go.

Every move is agony, but I'm fucking floating right now, pumped full of adrenaline. I feel the wind in the few remaining hairs on my scalp, feel the cool droplets of air smashing against my face. Even Gerald looks surprised as he continues swaying from the crossbar, eyes growing wide on my approach. Before he knows what's happening, I wrap my arms around his legs, sending us both crashing into the back of the net.

The crowd goes wild.

He begins raking at my face, but I'm on top with the advantage. There's a wildness in his eyes suggesting he means nothing but harm, but I thrust a knee into his chest and let my weight fall across him, all one hundred and thirty pounds of it. "You fucking cheat!" I scream, resisting his efforts to push me off. "You took my fucking leg out!"

"I'm going to put you in the fucking ground when I get up!" he cries.

He takes a swipe with his left, but I grab it out of thin air and pin it under my left knee. Face turning red, a strange and garbled croak leaving his lips; I know if he does get up, there's every chance he'll follow his threat through. "Get off me," he screams. "I'll fucking kill you!"

The noise of the crowd begins to fade, as do their faces. It's just him and me, a couple of crustaceans caught in the net, two old-timers fighting no longer for the damsel in front of us but the one underground, helping the daffodils grow.

"Get off me!" he cries from below. "What would Margie say?"

"Let me out of this fucking box, I imagine." I bring my fist into his cheek, his face registering surprise more than anything else. But Christ, I just hit him! I fucking hit a man! A terrible punch without a sound that made my fingers sing with pain, but still, it's the first time I've hit something not inanimate. His shock gives way to anger as he tries to force himself from the ground, spittle spraying from thin lips as he becomes frenzied, kicking out with his legs and swinging his free arm back and forth. I duck. I shimmy. But he catches me a good one on the nose, and my eyes begin to cloud. Another glancing blow across the top of my forehead momentarily stuns me, slowing time down.

"I think that's enough now, boys," someone's voice floats across. Not Elsie's, though; she's here to guzzle on the blood of the dead, it seems.

Gerald takes the opportunity to turn to his side, and I feel myself losing balance. "I'll fucking kill you!" he screams. I punch him again, harder this time, and it's a good connection that makes a satisfying noise against the bone, his teeth now resting on a patch of mud, three inches to his left.

"You're fudding dead!" He performs another shimmy that finally throws me off.

Momentarily, I'm staring at the moon, feeling the first few drops of rain against my skin. Only the sight of Gerald scrambling towards me, perfect teeth back in place and brandishing a metal goal peg in his right hand, snaps back into reality. I grab his wrist, and we lash out with our free hands, but he has the top position, and my blows feel weak, my arms already leaden.

"Boys!" someone cries, but the voice is distant, otherworldly.

I feel my nose snap, warmth filling my nostrils, bitterness at the back of my throat. His bulging eyes and menacing smile bear down on me, a string of saliva hanging from the overwhelming pinkness. Struggling to get my bearings, dazed and confused, Gerald breaks my grip and brings the peg down hard into my shoulder, forcing a garbled cry.

The crowd gasps, and some scream, but not one fucker steps in.

He's frenzied, past the point of no return. I see blood leaking across my shirt, the rain coming down harder now, aiding its spread. Offering an animalistic roar, a crazed Gerald brings the peg down even harder. Fuuuuucccccck! This time, it goes deeper, sending my nerve endings into overdrive.

Fight or flight. Fight or flight.

I reach behind me, grimacing as his makeshift weapon plunges into my side, setting fire to my insides. The silent crowd at their limit, I see their legs shuffling back; Gerald's hat resting on the no-mans-land between us.

"I think we should call the police," someone says. No shit!

Blow after blow, I feel metal piercing my flesh and exploring within. I hear screams leave my lips, but it all seems so fucking surreal; two old fogies writhing on the grass, like school kids in an after-school fight.

"I fucking hate you, Eric Smith!" he screams.

I continue trying to work one of the other goal pegs free as two of the crowd tentatively try and restrain Gerald, but he's rabid, at once laughing and snarling, a domesticised old man gone wild and ready to tear someone's face off. There's no doubt he means to kill me, and he's halfway there, relentless in his attack.

Finally, I manage to slide my finger under the cold metal and drag it from the ground. In a move that surprises even me, I spin that weapon around like Clint fucking Eastwood, close my eyes and blindly drive it upwards.

"My fucking eye," Gerald finally screams. "You've fucking blinded me!"

Feel warmth dripping onto my chin; I unscrew my eyes and take the opportunity, squirming on the ground and using what little strength I have to force him off. We continue lashing out as we fall to our sides, kicking, punching, sliding, growling, but I have the advantage, Gerald's left hand plugging his leaking eye. Still, my body screams at me to stop, pain lighting up every part of me, blood pooling beneath.

I'm no longer scared, though. For the first time in my life, I'm over the fucking wall.

I grab the net with my left hand and wrap my right around his throat, grimacing as metal finds my neck but fails to pierce my skin. Again and again, he strikes, but each attack grows weaker. Using my last ounce of strength, I simultaneously drag the net back as far as I can while pushing against his scrawny neck until I finally manage to squeeze his bald little head through one of the holes. Immediately, he starts clawing at the makeshift web, kicking his legs at the ground for leverage, but the grass is too wet for his poncy little brogues to get any traction, and soon he's exhausted, gasping for air.

"The things we did, Eric! Depraved. Filthy," he croaks. "And she always insisted on keeping the lights on." He continues his struggles, working at the net, a streak of stickiness running down his cheek. "You'll always be a fucking loser!"

I glance over my shoulder at the sound of sirens but only see the crowd—nothing more than silhouettes now. The rain intensifies, pattering fast and hard against my head, the accompanying wind gathering tempo.

"Always a fucking loser," he croaks.

Thinking it too good to resist, I drag myself towards the trilby, finally releasing a pained groan as I crouch and shake off the excess on its brim.

"Hey, that's my fucking hat!" he screams.

"Mine now." I put it on, giving the brim a flick—my turn to play cowboy.

"This is a fucking long way from over," he cries. But his struggles slow, and like a spider, I make my way towards the trapped prey.

Seventy-seven years old. Scared of my own shadow. A child and grandchild who visit less than infrequently because I have nothing interesting to say, just a wizened up empty shell of a man.

"You haven't got it in you, Eric! Once a loser."

A tattered book with no words.

"You're pathetic! A waste of a skeleton!"

One by one, I begin collecting the goal pegs, squinting into the hard rain.

"What are you doing?" he cries. "What the fuck are you doing?"

As I make my way towards him, the man I've hated for countless years, I hear the squeal of tyres and see the blur of red and blue reflecting on his face.

"No, don't! Eric, don't you fucking—"

The scream is instant and high-pitched as I plunge one of the pegs into his remaining eye, almost managing to drown out the now impossible to ignore sirens. I bring the next one into his shoulder. The next into his neck. Again and again, I strike, forcing a series of high-pitched cries as blood spreads rapidly across his yellow shirt, creating a quite beautiful tapestry.

"I'm the one she came back to, Gerald," I say through gritted teeth, down to my last peg.

He offers a half-assed growl, writhing against the net and clawing at his throat and eyes, but soon his protests quieten to a series of dampened whimpers. Behind me, voices get louder, but there ain't no going back.

"Apologise, Gerald."

"Fuuuuuuuuuck youuuuuuuuuuu!"

And relentlessly, I begin bringing the peg down, over and over and over, until my arms burn and my fingers scream. I hit bone, gristle, sometimes it goes clean through and deep, creating individual rivers of red, until hardly a patch of yellow remains on his collar. After all these years, all those nasty, evil thoughts, the monster is finally out, and it feels so damned good. Offering a roar, I lift my arm back, ready to strike again, but the impossibly loud crack seems to stop time.

My first thought is lightning, striking perhaps just a few hundred yards away. But to the sound of distant screams, everything goes numb, and I crumple to the deceivingly hard ground.

More shouting emerges, drowning out Gerald's fading death gurgles. I hear the stomping of feet, taking me back to better times in the pub. "Sweet Caro—line. Dum-dum-dum-dum." The words come out as a rasp as I feel the wave of blackness approaching.

Basking in the dimming light of the full moon, I offer a weak howl and begin to laugh.

Finally, I have a story.

My name is Eric Smith. I'm seventy-seven years old, and I killed a man for sleeping with my wife.

"It's your round, Bernie," I say, removing the hat and holding it to my bleeding chest. "Margie, I'll try and do better this time."

A Low Spirit

Under the moonlight, the raven's feathers gleam like fresh paint-work. It watches curiously as my hands claw at the ground. I am getting nowhere. A single tear spills down my cheek, and the cool breeze accentuates its path, but it never makes it to the earth beneath.

I only have myself to blame.

The bird lifts its head, and its beady eyes offer no consolation for my guilt. I sit back on the damp ground and reflect on how it came to this.

She used to be so good with the children. It's hard to watch them struggle and hurt in the way they do. Lucy is having nightmares again, and the words I offer do little to comfort. She's always been a worrier, asking questions that should never be on a young child's mind, "Do you still love Mummy?"; "Why do you get sad?"; "Why does Mummy cry sometimes?"

It's Tom I worry about most though. He is not talking at all. I walked in on him a few days ago and caught him crying into his pillow.

On his drawing pad on the bedside table, there was a picture of the four of us holding hands and smiling.

I feel helpless, even more so sat here in the middle of the cemetery when I should be at home with the children. I bid farewell to the raven perched atop the stonework and set off home.

I want her back. I want to hold her and have another go at making her happy. We used to be.

The first time I saw her, I knew I wanted to be with her—intelligent, altruistic, complex, generous and very stubborn—my ever so stubborn English Rose. I loved her.

Our friends were shocked at how we would speak to each other at times, but I don't think they ever truly understood how comfortable we felt in each other's presence. We would joke and roast like best friends, love like adulterers and talk all night about anything under the sun. That seems like such a long time ago now.

A streetlight casts its warm glow on our house, but inside the light dwindles and it only makes it up the first three steps of the staircase. I creep up the boards slowly, half expecting a loud creak and subsequent cry from Lucy, but the house remains mute.

I pass the photo on the wall that portrays a lie. It is a recent one of Anne on her fortieth, trying to smile as though she had forgotten how. Depression had finally rooted itself. Pangs of guilt wash over me again as I run my finger over her forced smile. The make-up helps disguise the sleepless nights and taut face, but the eyes offer nothing but despondence.

The isolation was unbearable, and I know that comes across as selfish, but I was trying to hold everything together. After a while, I felt the cracks appear. My work was suffering, I was snappy at Lucy and Tom, and I used to get so frustrated with Anne. On occasions,

I felt so rigid with rage; I feared what might happen. Those times I would drive to the beach and cry or scream or both.

She seemed so adamant on self-destruction. I tried, but there is only so much you can do on your own. Admittedly, I was afraid to tap into that part of her mind—it would be like trying to defuse a bomb and if you didn't know which wires to cut...boom!

She had battled waves of it over the years. Sometimes it would last days and sometimes weeks, but she had always managed to fight her way out in the end. It was exhausting for both of us, and I couldn't help but feel that sometimes I made it worse. I used to think perhaps if she was with someone else, they could help her unlock the unshakable sadness that I couldn't.

My patience grew thin over time, and I shamefully started to throw around desperate ultimatums, threatening to leave and to take the kids. I couldn't reach her. She would happily take the drugs, but not the advice, and the pills she had started taking encouraged even more disconnect.

Gently, I stroke Lucy's cheek. She looks peaceful now, and I hope some light is getting through to her dreams. I want to scoop her up and squeeze her. She kept me going through a lot of the hard times, and I feel as though I have let her down too.

I peek into Tom's room and see the drawing of the four of us still sat on his table. He is curled up in a ball as though in self-protection mode and he looks so small and vulnerable. I want to wake him up and tell him everything is going to be okay. I kiss him on the forehead and whisper I love him before moving to our room.

I wanted a happy ending, back to where we used to be—I begged her countless times to see someone.

I had nothing left to give at the end.

The dresser that used to be packed to the brim with bottles of colourful tablets is now almost empty apart from the ripped open envelope and letter cast aside. I have read that first line so many times now.

Dear Mrs. Jones

This is to confirm your booking with psychologist Dr. Lauper on 17th September at 10 am.

There is a small groan behind me, and I turn to look at my wife in bed and watch her until she settles once again.

The envelope is postmarked the 4th of September, the day before I locked myself in the garage with the engine running. She never said a word. Maybe she was frightened of failure.

I will never forgive myself. The raven has watched me helplessly claw at my grave many times—punishment enough, perhaps.

The end

Nocturnal Pursuits of the Elderly

Saturday night, finally.

It seemed to take forever to come around.

I can hardly bear it, my head buzzing like a kid's on Christmas Eve, goosebumps dancing across my leathery skin. "Usual time, pet?"

"Please, dear. And don't forget to feed Alfred."

"Never do, dear. Never do." Now off you fuck, darling.

"And there's some quiche wrapped in the fridge, Marty. It needs eating."

Quiche, my arse. Kiss my arse. I'm just a child wrapped in a silly old costume. "Yes, dear. Now go on; the bridge crowd will be waiting." I'll get at least three hours with her, perhaps more.

She steps out of the car and leans over, giving me her gummy smile. Who'd have thought someone could get so giddy over a few glasses of cheap wine and a game of cards?

"Have fun, love," I say. "Don't get too wild."

It made her day when they let her join a few years ago; picky apparently about who they let in. I've only ever met Jon—installed the security system and sensors throughout both houses—shy as a schoolgirl, he was. Nice enough, I suppose.

Ah, there she goes, my dearest Susan, her oversized handbag clutched between her knobbly fingers. As she hobbles up the driveway, I offer a wave. She doesn't get out much, bless her, and happy wife, happy life, and all that. Forty years on Tuesday, the majority of them peaceful.

And... we're off.

It's hard adhering to speed limits when urgency flows through your veins, but I don't like to tempt fate. These nights are special, ones to be savoured, and every second counts. I wind the window down, enjoying the breeze and smell of the night that fills me with nostalgic melancholy. Long summer evenings on our bikes, legs going like the clappers as though we could escape the inevitable darkness. I offer a commemorative howl to the already visible larger-than-life three-quarter moon.

Damn, I love Saturdays.

Forecaster said there's a heatwave coming, but for now, coolness caresses me, going some way to calm my nerves. Sinatra sings his smoothness on the radio, too, but some punk DJ with no right to fade the master out starts spitting out words, spreading mould. So much bad news. Local politicians and their barefaced lies, homeless numbers going through the roof, and an influx of drugs in the area. And beware, the full moon killer is still at large and will likely strike again next week. Please make sure you report any suspicious behaviour to your local police station. Have a pleasant evening, friends.

The changeover track kicks in, some one-hit-wonder from the eighties.

As I roll up the driveway, Alfred spies me, immediately starting to rub himself against the door, tail eloquently swishing with expectation. Susan's pride and joy, fur as soft as the night sky, but a privileged little fucker I have no time for. Put a cat flap in the tradesman's entrance, but the stupid little hairy bastard still insists on using the front door.

Offering next door's bedroom window a glance, I get out of the car and breathe in more of the evening. Ah, to be young again. "Get out of it," I say, sweeping my foot across the front step, just missing Alfred's behind. He retreats behind Susan's greying horned statue of whatever-the-fuck that is, but by the time I close the door, his distorted and annoying face is back at the frosted glass, offering a forgiving and hopeful meow.

"Go play with the traffic."

We've lived here for over thirty years now. Back in '97, we decided to split the house and rent next door out. We figured it would be worth the initial cost if we could get a decent return, and being a builder myself, we came well within budget. Even converted both lofts into makeshift studios, skylights and all. Best decision we ever made, taking some financial pressure away and meaning we could retire early.

It gave me a whole new lease of life, too.

Walking almost too fast for my arthritic legs, I head towards the kitchen and grab the quiche from the fridge. Quiche my arse.

Guilt? A little.

But we've all got our skeletons, secret fantasies, and dark areas of our minds to which only we have the map. And don't come over all innocent with me; nobody is without a vice.

"Here you go, you little shit," I say to Alfred, sliding the generous slice across the step. "A word of this to Susan, and I'll fuck you up, okay?"

Alfred meows and strokes himself against me like a two-bit male hooker.

"Glad we understand each other. Now eat the shitty quiche." I can't ever remember telling Susan that I liked it, but I don't have the heart to tell her I don't.

Almost falling up the stairs, my breathing becomes fast and erratic, accompanied by a stirring down below and an involuntary squeal. In our bedroom, the familiar heavy scent of my wife's body butter awaits, as does the obscene number of illuminated amateur sculptures on the corner dressing table, the ones she makes in the studio—half-human, half-animal, all garbage. Still, as I work at the secret panel of the closet, my adrenaline overrides anything but thoughts of my Charlotte.

There it is. Beautiful.

Limb by limb, I squeeze myself into it, the PVC suit squeaking its indecent soundtrack. Finally, I begin zipping it over my belly.

Gloves next. And now, the leather mask.

Alas, I'm a creature of the night, invisible, stealthy, leaving no trace.

I feel charged, but I remind myself a costume is just a costume as I stagger down the stairs. There's even a temptation to jump the last few, as I used to when my legs were more than just solidified dust. Thoughts of Susan coming home and finding me broken at the bottom of the steps, head to toe in leather, dissuade flight. I doubt she would believe I was playing at being Batman.

A cold draught swallows me as I open the basement door, bringing with it a sharpness of alcohol, the only other hobby of mine. I flick on the light and carefully navigate the concrete steps, running my leather-clad fingers across the smoothness of the stone.

Beetroot, turnip, celery; it's incredible what you can make good wine from. Susan's not a fan of the stuff, but I believe having different interests is healthy, especially when there's an empty nest. She's got her bridge club, pottery, and plenty of books about gemstones and animals, even those weird ones under the bed that she thinks I don't know about. I like making liquor and, well, let's call them other after-hours pursuits.

This space always feels larger than it is, likely down to what I know or possibly just the airiness of it. I added alcoves into the wall as a nice touch, bottles of my latest batches sitting proudly within.

Aways takes a few tries to locate. "Come on, where are—"

The secret door swings inwards, revealing the almost empty utility shelf on the other side. I put it together before handing over the keys, thinking it would be a nice little touch for further camouflage. It's been standing for over two decades, just another example of my craft.

One more screw and—clear.

And into the makeshift laundry I go, the one I helped do the plumbing for. Charlotte was so grateful at the time. Said I was "a genius." Giddy with anticipation, I make my way up the steps.

Inhale. Exhale. Inhale.

And with a satisfying click of the handle, I'm in.

A strange and familiar feeling washes over me, a euphoric combination of anticipation, desire, and homeliness. Everything is different, softer, like a mini vacation to somewhere new. Much more than voyeurism, we have a special bond. I've spoken to her, made her laugh, fixed the downstairs toilet, mowed her lawn, and poured her a glass of beetroot wine on her patio. I'm part of her life, breathing her air, inhaling her molecules of perfume, a floral and seductive concoction that tickles the back of my throat.

"I'm home, Charlotte."

This is more like a relationship, you see. I'm the man of this—these—houses.

You may mock, but I've even seen her play with her hair when she talks to me, the blood rushing to her face. Seen the losers she dates, too; nowhere near good enough for her. One guy lasted a few months, but I soon put paid to that, sneaking into the bedroom on three occasions and cleaning out his wallet. Pissed all over the bathroom floor, too. There's a new guy on the scene now, but he won't last if I have anything to do with it. He's only stayed over three times that I know of, but that's more than enough. I dropped into town last week and picked up a lacy pair of red panties. Now, if they should accidentally happen into the pocket of his overly tight pants.

The giant television screen casts my glossy and smooth reflection as I flop onto the couch. Perhaps it's why I like wearing the extra skin, to cover the imperfections that age brings, and to match the youthfulness of my mind and all the desires that refuse to relent.

I've still got so much to offer, but Susan knocks back my advances. Just because I'm getting on a bit doesn't mean I don't have urges. That said, it's never my wife I imagine beneath me, always Charlotte, her low-cut dress up to her waist, hands on my buttocks, bringing me into her.

Make love to me, Marty. Make me feel!

Love should have no boundaries, age or otherwise. And it is love; I know it is. We'd do it properly. I'd tell Susan first, and then we could escape to the country and stay in a B&B for a while until we decided the next steps.

Just keep telling yourself that, Marty.

I reach over, tonguing the rim of the wine glass smeared with lipstick, before sipping some of the remaining wine and swirling it around in my mouth. Earthiness, cherries, raspberry. It's a Pinot-Noir, not top shelf, but none of that cheap crap either.

There's so much I could teach her about wine. We could spend the weekend in France, the country of love, where anything goes, with no boundaries left to break.

"J'adore ton sourire."

As I push myself up, I notice three boxes in the corner of the room and make my way over. One has the word charity scrawled across the side, full of clothes, ornaments, and DVDs. The other two are un-marked and full of books, everything from Twilight to Dale Carnegie. She must be having a clear-out of sorts.

Untidiness greets me in the kitchen, lots of stuff scattered across the counter. Sometimes I do a bit of a clean-up, not being a fan of slovenliness, but it all depends on how the night rolls. The fridge has nothing of much interest, although I can't resist fingering a dollop of cream from the mini birthday cake. Thirty-two candles squished in there, someone having a shitty sense of humour. I wrote her a poem for her birthday, and I'll read it to her one day.

The smell of perfume gets even stronger as I make my way up the stairs. No need to avoid the creak of the fourth step; that's only a factor when she's still in the house. I must admit, those sorts of visits are becoming more regular, but before you start judging, I don't get up to no funny business. I just sit in the plush chair, watching and listening: The gentle rise and fall of her smooth chest, the little moans as she changes position. Okay, once I did climb onto the bed, nestling behind her, inhaling and sucking on strands of her long brown hair. But I didn't feel so good about it. Drew a line right there and then.

I'm not one of those pervert types, I assure you.

As I cross the threshold to her bedroom, I'm transported to that now familiar and different world, a mellow heaven full of dizzying scents. "Oh, Charlotte." I pull back the sheets of the bed, take off my mask and work at the zipper of my suit. Filled with anticipation, I let myself fall into softness, my tongue lapping at the linen, my bare chest slaking across her nest. Drawing back the sheets over my shoulders, I squirm with delight, imagining her naked form doing the same.

"Nearly five years strong now, I knew you were the one. The others meant nothing. Fell in love with you as soon as I saw you, my dear Charlotte."

As I said, I'd leave Susan for her if that's what it came down to. Forty years of marriage just for one night with my true love.

My eyes fall across the linen basket.

I do try. Really. Every Saturday night after returning home, I convince myself it will never happen again, but the pull is too strong. It's not just a sexual thing; it makes me feel closer to her, the smell and taste lingering long after I remove the panties from around my face.

I'm not a pervert, okay!

Besides, nothing should be forbidden between lovers.

I remove the ones shoved down the side of the suit and slide them into the edge of the basket, collecting the fresh ones on the way out. Almost immediately, I feel the blood running to my—

"The fuck?"

Headlights leak through the window, the accompanying engine louder still.

No, that can't be. She's never home before eleven.

Holding my breath, I run to the window, heart pounding as I watch Charlotte's ten-year-old Audi come to a halt, a small rental van pulling close behind.

Shit! Shit. Shit!

Doors open. Voices emerge. Him. It's him with the tidy hair and tight arse who normally rolls up in the Mercedes.

I'll never make it.

My grip on the panties tightens as I watch them embrace. "This isn't right."

As they make their way to the door, I search the room, opting for the closet and regretting it immediately. Cursing myself for having no contingency plan, I feel like a sitting duck in a PVC suit.

Fuck it all!

I hear laughter. And the creak of the fourth step.

"It will be dark soon, Patrick," she says. "We really should make a start."

"It's all about the preparation, Charlie. Slowly, softly, catchy monkey."

Charlie? That's not her fucking name, Bozo. I press my back against the wood of the closet, sliding a dress across for further concealment.

They're in the bedroom now, undressing. This is a fucking nightmare. The love of my life, and him. She doesn't even notice the unmade bed as she's thrown across it. He drops to his knees, wrestling with her panties. Tainted, those, no good to me.

Please let this end.

He goes in for the kill, feasting on her deliciousness, the full course, not just an appetiser. Fucking hate him! The noises. Christ, the noises. I squirm against the wood, holding my breath at the accompanying squeak.

Even playing fucking bridge would be better than enduring this.

He moves on top of her, wrapping his mouth around her now-exposed nipple. "Our very own place, Patrick. I can't believe it," she says. He offers a moan of approval, wrestling with his belt.

I still love you, Charlotte. We'll fix this.

His pants drop to the floor. And the shirt.

His moans get louder, breathing too, and soon he is thrashing into her as though she's a sack of potatoes. I can't watch; it's too much.

Reciprocating the groans, poor Charlotte does her best to pretend she's enjoying it, but how could she be?

I edge forwards, sliding my feet to the front of the closet. It has to be smooth, or the game is up.

The bed begins to shake wildly, scraping against the wall.

Oh, Charlotte, why do you cheapen yourself?

Three.

Bang.

Two.

Bang

One.

Bang.

I make my move, wincing at the feedback from my arthritic legs as I drop to the floor and scramble towards the crumpled heap of clothes. After shoving the black panties in my mouth, I slip my hand into my suit and pull out the red ones.

Here goes nothing.

Her moans grow louder still as she does her best to keep him happy.

Why, Charlotte? Why?

Time to go.

Crossing over the threshold into the hallway, I get to my feet with a grimace and glance over my shoulder, only to see them still entwined in debauchery. Like fucking animals, they are. That's not love; where's the tenderness? And so much for slowly, slowly, catchy monkey, the pervert's going at it like a jackhammer.

Wondering what happened to real love, I bring the panties to my face and inhale. All is well until visions of them invade my head, tainting those sheets I was nestled within only a few minutes ago. Tears fill my eyes as I close the basement door and make my way up the steps.

We'd be happy; I know it.

Susan? I love her, too, just in a different way. Besides, she shows the cat more affection than me. I get lonely, see. I might be over the hill, my face wearing life and too much sun, but I still miss the tender touch of a female.

And under my fucking roof!

Feeling lightheaded and out of breath, I pause halfway up. Their groans fill my head, violently bouncing around, just like the bed. Bang. Bang. Bang. It's enough to drive a man insane.

Inhale.

Just a mistake; we all make mistakes.

Exhale.

She'll regret it in the morning.

It comes as an unusual relief to close the basement door behind me. "Oh, Charlotte." Trying to give her the benefit of the doubt, I slump into the living room couch and unzip. In a well-practiced fashion, I drag the panties across my nipples and slide them downwards my crotch. I'm semi-aroused but can't bring myself to go any further. He's in my head. The fucking-fucker! The neat-haired, tight-arsed fuckity-fuck!

My Charlotte is moving out; I can't believe it. She's leaving me without so much as a word. I knew we shouldn't have let her pay by the month.

After a couple more whiskies, I hear voices. Tears filling my eyes, I creep towards the bay window and watch from behind the nets as they carry her stuff into that shitty little van. Finally, with one last look back at the place, they drive off into the distance.

Oh, Charlotte.

Angrily, I wrap the panties around my head and fall onto the couch.

Another whisky.

And another.

Finally, after several minutes of sobbing and drinking, the tidal wave of exhaustion wins its battle.

It takes a while to realise where I am, the blue flashing to my left prompting me to reach out, knocking the tumbler to the ground. Shitfuck! "Hello?" Ah, shit. I aim for the green button again. "Hello?"

"It's me, Marty. It's 10.30. Where are you?"

"Ah, Christ. I'm so sorry, love. I—I fell asleep... Yes, I'll be there in five... Can't you wait inside?... Yes, okay, I'm on my way... Sorry, love... Yes, I said I'm sorry."

Fuck-a-duck.

On my second attempt, I thrust myself from the couch towards the door. It's not until I'm halfway down the driveway I realise I'm leather-clad with panties stuck to my face. Fuck it to Hell and back! Snapping my head up and down the street, I rush inside and slam the door shut behind me. Come on. Come on. It takes what feels like inhuman strength to peel off the suit, and by the time I'm out, I'm dripping with sweat and can hardly breathe.

Worst night ever.

Using the banister, I drag myself upstairs and shove the PVC costume back behind the panel. But true love never runs smoothly. The same temptation to jump the last few stairs washes over me as I urgently slip an arm through my shirt. Finally, I'm out the door, decent but exhausted and heartbroken.

Slightly cooler evening air rushes through the window, but I have the smell of sweaty PVC embedded in my nostrils. Fortunately, Susan couldn't smell a fart if it slapped her on both cheeks. Traffic lights blur, the dotted white line becoming solid as I drive slightly over the speed limit, a first for everything, but I hate to think of her standing outside alone. She's still my Susan.

There she is. I give her a flash, and she offers a wave and a smile. God bless her.

"Good night, love?" I say jovially.

"Have you been crying, Marty?"

"No, it's the wind. Was it fun?"

"Always," she says, fixing her hair in the mirror. "Did you enjoy the peace?"

"I did up to a point," I reply, pulling away, "and then I started missing you."

"Liar. Is that whisky on your breath?"

"Just a little hot toddy, love," I reply, noticing how strongly I'm gripping the wheel. "How is everyone?"

"Very well." She winds the window down and swallows the breeze. "They always ask after you."

I clear my throat. "Saw a removal van next door tonight. Hasn't even given notice."

"Charlotte? She came to see me last week. Moving in with that man with the tidy hair."

"But they've only been out a few times." I lower my tone. "To be young and stupid, eh?"

"She seems quite smitten." She reaches for my hand and squeezes. "I said I'd go and give her a hand on Tuesday. Make the tea and help her organise. Her man is out of town, coming down with the big truck on Wednesday morning."

I'm her man. "But Tuesday's our anniversary?"

"Well, you'll just have to cancel those tickets for Paris you booked then, won't you? Besides, I've organised a little shindig for us in the evening. I think it's about time you met the bridge club. Nothing fancy, just some wine and canapes. Jennifer said—"

Her words grow distant, my mind back on Charlotte, full of nostalgic melancholy, memories of our times together, all playing to a soundtrack of pained voices and heart-breaking chords. Part of me is tempted to say I'll go with her to help, but I know it would be too much. Just the thought of saying goodbye to her—ah, this is all so fucking unbearable.

I spend the rest of the night trying to hide my sadness, but I know Susan picks up on it. Half-expecting an inquisition, she just keeps looking at me and smiling. God bless her.

The next few days continue much the same way. I do my best, but sometimes I have to leave the room, biting my lip to fight back the tears. Susan leaves me be, but I know she'd be there for me if needed. By the time Tuesday comes around, I've written thirteen poems and a top forty list of the saddest songs from my LP collection.

Just because I'm old doesn't mean I don't feel.

Through the bay window, I see Charlotte's brown curls and the smile across her face that I know won't last. Not with him. She slams the car door shut and skips towards the front door, disappearing behind the hedgerow.

"Going over there now, love," Susan says from the front of the house. "There's another quiche for you on the top shelf of the fridge. Oh, and listen out for the door, will you?"

Poor fucking Alfred. "Wait! How long are you planning—" The door slams shut. Christ, the thought of facing guests is unbearable; all the fake smiles and superficial chatter when my heart is bleeding.

I spend the day alternating between pacing the room and flopping on the couch, occasionally picking up the crossword and just staring at it. She's in my head. The scent, the smile, the laugh. The panties. But I'm even too heartbroken to consider pleasuring myself. I have no appetite either, but I make sure Alfred gets a generous slice of the soppy mess in the fridge just because I hate him so fucking much.

Early afternoon already. What the hell are they doing across there?

I take to pacing again, thinking back to the time we spent together in the dark, moonlight falling across her cheek. Oh, how I longed to kiss those soft, youthful lips, slide my fingers into the negligée, and caress her warmth. I'm a hopeless romantic, nourished by thoughts of walks on the beach and rolling in the sand. Another bout of tears threatens to release, prompting me to curl my fingers into a fist.

Tomorrow she will be out of my life, for good.

The afternoon is swallowed by a black hole of grief and despair, the eventual knock at the door tempting me to scramble behind the couch. But I know Susan has gone to some trouble, and that, somehow, I need to snap myself out of this stupor and stop being so damned selfish.

Four of the dullest-looking wrinklies I've ever seen await on the other side of the door: Two men and two women. It looks as though they were all made from the same lacklustre mould. Pale and greying skin, downturned mouths, prominent hanging jowls, and eyes like flooded marsh ground. Christ, is this what I look like to Charlotte?

"Hello."

Nobody replies as they begin shuffling past me, little bags in one hand and a covered serving dish in the other, placing them on the table as they pass. Mouth agape, I watch them trudge through the living room to begin lining up outside the basement door like albino lemmings. "Excuse me," I say, but another tap at the door steals my attention.

More of them. Another six clones, all with little bags and more dishes. I recognise Jon at the back of the group only because of his lopsided face and twitch in his right eye.

"Jon."

"Marty."

It's an absurd situation, and my head, already in bits, struggles to comprehend any of it. Before I can even string a sentence together, my phone vibrates.

"Susan, what the hell is—... Yes, ten of them... What?... I'm not in the mood for this, Susan; please tell me what is happening... Yes, of course I love you... Yes, I trust you... Oh Christ... But—but—... How? Ah, pet, I'm sorry, I—... No... I don't know what came over—... What? You can't be serious?... Susan, I... Yes, alright, alright... Yes, I'll do it... Okay... I'll see you in an hour."

Shit! How much does she know?

Drone number one turns the handle, and the others follow him down into the basement. As the last grey-face crosses the threshold into my other world, I replay the conversation with Susan in my head. She knows about the suit. How? And what's all this about an anniversary present? I follow the already flattened tread in the carpet, performing more laps, occasionally stopping to fill my tumbler with whisky, and eventually scampering upstairs to wrestle with the suit. It takes an eternity in the heat to squeeze into it.

What the fuck is going on?

Everything seems so futile now my Charlotte is leaving me, but this, this is the icing on the cake. How can I ever look my wife in the eye?

The phone rings again, and I tentatively answer it, feeling as though I may internally combust at any moment. "Yes, dear... Okay dear... On my way dear. And I'm so—"

The excitement I usually feel walking down the stairs is replaced with trepidation and an ominous sense of finality. Susan and her friends have trespassed into my world, and I'm about to establish why.

I reach the last few steps to find the secret door already ajar, and the shelf on the other side unscrewed and slid across. How the hell?

"Susan?"

Walking into next door's basement, I get a faint whiff of familiarity. But something else, too. A spicy, smoky concoction. Is that music? Ascending the concrete steps towards the warm yellow light makes my stomach churn.

"Susan?"

At the top of the stairs, the music is louder still.

"Susan!"

I approach the ever-increasing noise, noting the gemstones leading further into the house and up the staircase. And what's that? Sounds like moaning. Or muffled cries? Legs feeling like lead weights, I take the steps one by one, my nostrils filling with more of that heavy sweetness. "Susan!" Before I reach the top, I notice the ladder to the attic pulled down and the gentle sway of the ceiling light. More prolonged groans emerge, and what the hell is that slapping sound?

At the top of the landing, I arch my neck towards the shifting light above. A candle? "Susan!" My heart pounds as I clasp my hands around the cold steel. One step at a time, I begin the ascent, blood pounding in my ears, almost surprised my legs support me. Above me, heavy breathing, squeaking, squelching, pounding. An acrid sweaty smell begins to fall across me, above and beyond what was there before.

Something horrible lies beyond that rectangular portal; I know it.

Finally, I emerge, almost losing my footing as I take in the savagery surrounding me. I see a lion, deer, cat, panther, leopard, even a fucking lobster, grunting, thrusting, bending, a twisted jungle of surrealness coming at me from all directions. I place my hands down for balance, my fingers brushing against the cold plastic sheet that appears to run the loft's full length, there only, I imagine, to catch whatever juices drip.

"Happy anniversary," my wife says between pants, but I haven't a clue which one she is. "Your present's in the corner."

"What the fuck is going on, Susan?"

"Oh, come on, Marty," she says, ripping the cat mask off. I should have guessed. "We've all seen what you get up to after lights out."

"What? What are you talking about?" Oh, Christ.

"Nocturnal pursuits? Her knickers stuffed in your mouth, running around her bedroom dressed in leather, beating your chest like Tarzan." Groaning turns to cackles. "It's okay, though, dear," she continues. "We like what we like." The lion behind carries on pounding into her, offering a roar.

"How? How did you—"

"Cameras all over, dear. Courtesy of Jon when he did the alarm system. You can't be too careful in a neighbourhood like this."

Her comments prompt more laughter. The lion is no longer a lion, back to a pale-faced twitching drone with the mask tucked under his arm, sweat dripping down both cheeks and splashing against the plastic sheet. "Hi, Marty," he says.

"Is this what it would take, Susan? Before you would touch me? For me to dress up like a fucking animal."

She looks me up and down and smiles. "I've decided I want to share this with you, Marty. The others weren't sure about letting you in, said we should both have our own interests, but I think this might be good for us. Exciting. We can go out with a bang. Fuck like we did in the old days."

A different cry emerges from behind her, heightening my adrenaline even further. I heave myself up, weaving my way between the animals towards the back of the room. "Charlotte?" She's bound to the radiator; someone's gigantic underpants shoved down her throat. She looks at me with pleading eyes, mascara running down both cheeks.

My Charlotte.

I crouch down, running my fingers through her hair, goosebumps prickling my skin within a skin. Her eyes are glassy and delayed, her lips as soft as I remember.

"I know how much you like this one," Susan says, pulling herself away from the lion-lemming hybrid. She holds her back as she creases towards the floor and picks up a knife. "Happy Anniversary," she says, offering me the handle and a peck on the cheek.

I drop my gaze to the trembling blade. "What am I supposed to do with this?"

"Full moon, Marty. It's a special night, made even more special by our anniversary. The group has accepted you into the flock. Everything is aligned."

"You want me to use this on her?" Full moon killer still at large.

"Nourish yourself. Feed on her blood, and forever immortalise your bond. She's our sacrifice to the animal gods."

All those books under her side of the bed, the ones on animal worship and ancient rituals, all those twisted fucking things staring at us under the moonlight. "People don't get away with stuff like this."

"His fingerprints are on the knife, Marty. They're everywhere. We've already sent a message from her phone saying she no longer believes him about the panties. Nice touch, by the way."

"This is insane." But I'm as hard as rock.

"He's on his way. At least two hours to go. And we're all each other's alibi; bridge night at our house. Full spread, the works. Just old codgers enjoying what time is left, having our night disturbed by the shouting and screaming next door."

I feel young again, a kid on a dare, more aroused than I can ever remember being. And this woman, this stranger; I can't help feeling like I'm falling in love with my wife all over again. "You do this every week?"

"We only kill on a full moon, Marty." She smiles. "Mostly the homeless, druggies, street filth, doing our bit to keep the neighbourhood tidy. The rest of the time, we just fuck like animals."

I lean in towards Charlotte, inhaling her hair and perfume, but there's a residue of something else—of him.

"Said she was relieved to be moving," my wife says. "Said that she didn't feel safe here anymore. Things moving, going missing, and sometimes as though she was being watched. Said the area was going downhill, too. I guess that's gratitude for you."

Charlotte issues another muffled plea, but Susan's words have me reeling. Everything I did for her—the chores, tidying up, mowing the goddamn lawns. I feel cheated. Let down. Used. Regardless, I lean in, the salty sweat of her forehead soaking into my thin, dry lips.

Our first proper kiss, and I know, our last.

But all I can think of is the trouble Susan has gone to. For me. And all I got her was a box of chocolates and a shitty card. "I don't know what to say, Suse."

"You're welcome," my wife replies.

As I slide the knife an inch-deep into Charlotte's chest, and her muffled cries heighten to a sobbing crescendo, I feel charged, horny beyond belief. Blood cascades between us, and I rub it frantically across my face and chest and lick it from her wound. Soon the others join, like animals at a waterhole, lapping up the magnificent red, fighting and fucking for the best spot. Writhing on the floor, Charlotte reaches out to me, but our fling is over; I have a marriage to work on. And she can watch for a change.

Thirst quenched, I borrow pasty's mane and fuck my wife in the corner with as much vigour as I can manage for a man of sixty-seven.

It turns out I am a cat person, after all.

"Go again, Susan?"

As she purrs, I howl at the moon framed in the skylight.

SPOONS

"I see he's out there again."

"Didn't even eat breakfast," Sheila says. "Got him Fruit Loops, too."

"I don't think that kind of food helps, love; all those e-numbers and whatnot."

Sheila crunches down on her toast, observing her husband's ever-growing belly, doubting he could pick a courgette from a cucumber. Renowned paediatrician, Doctor Geoff, sporting his stretched and threadbare underpants and flaunting advanced terminologies such as e-numbers and whatnot. She bites her tongue. "There's some leftover cake in the fridge if you want it?"

"Oh, aye, love, I won't say no to that." He leans towards the window, giving his chest a good old scratch, studying the holes in their once manicured garden. "The look on his face. Such intensity. Shame he doesn't clean his room with such aggression."

It's not as though Sheila's stopped worrying about her son, but there comes the point, just like grief, she supposes, that one has to start letting go, or at least try. Every morning Sam greets her with his melt-your-heart smile, eyes wide and hungry, and who is she to deny him one of the few things that thrills and excites him.

"Christ, there's not a single spoon that isn't bent," Geoff says, raking through the cutlery drawer. He finally gives up, putting the cake plate down and bending one back in place. "It's like living with Uri-friggin-Geller."

"The astronaut?"

"No, you daft bugger, that fella that could bend spoons."

Her gaze still on her husband, Sheila's mind begins flicking through all the sessions with the so-called professionals. Autism. ADHD. So many terms liberally coined but offering no real resolution, just words she could use for inquisitive friends and family to justify his stimming and lack of engagement. Her sister would never believe any of it, always insisting it was just part of the boy's personality. She died thinking it, too.

"You alright, love?"

"Yeah, I'm fine. As long as he's happy, I'm happy."

He reaches for her hand and squeezes it. "Hey, look on the bright side. At least it was a cheap birthday this year; forty packs of Cost Cutter spoons and the remastered box set of Indiana Jones."

She nods, watching Geoff sink the misshapen spoon into the icing. "In hindsight, we should have kept a pack for ourselves."

Geoff smiles. "If he ever asks for a shovel, we're fucked."

In the yard, humming the theme tune to Indiana Jones, Sam works his way through dry soil. His palm stings, and his fingers ache, but he knows he must be getting closer, this being the only patch of grass not yet savaged. The familiar scent of laundry liquid fills his nostrils as the cool morning breeze blows across, shadows of the washing above proving frustrating as light becomes dark becomes light. Further down the street, he hears children playing and dogs barking, but shrillness only temporarily overrides the familiar voices in his head.

The buzzing has always been there, the background hum. He can never remember the name of what his mum calls it, but only since moving into the house a few months ago did it transition to voices. Female. Children, he thinks. The pair speak in perfect synchronicity leading Sam to suspect they may be twins. Weak and distant once, the voices become stronger with each passing day, and from the moment his eyes open to when they close, they are with him.

"Harvey, stop it!"

He's always been different, he knows it—all those fancy offices and smarmy smiles—but this place has finally given him a focus, a mission. Something awaits here, and it's calling to him. A connection that only he is picking up.

And the things he's been promised.

He grits his teeth and stabs the spoon into the ground, but the already weakened handle gives. "Fuck off, Harvey!" he yells to the dog as it nuzzles for attention. "I'm on a mission here." The dog finally saunters to the other side of the garden, dropping to the superman position under the shade of the rose bush and letting out a sigh.

"I'm sorry, Harvs," he mutters, "but I'm close; I know it." He tosses the now useless implement behind him and grabs another from the pile.

Shadows grow shorter. Spoons bend. Harvey finally retires inside, the heat getting too much for him.

A potent concoction of sun cream and sweat streaming down his forehead, Sam alternates digging hands, face crumpled as he rubs relentlessly at his eyes, producing a series of marshy squeaks. Regardless, he continues to dig, his vision blurry and stinging; the cheese sandwich his mum brought out half an hour ago remaining untouched bar the small army of ants.

"Oh, God. Indy, this is it! This is it!"

He bites at his lip, stabbing frantically at the surrounding ground. His heart rate is up, hairs prickling across his body, adrenaline numbing the pain. Stab. Stab. Stab. Scrape. Scrape. Scrape. Stab. Stab. Stab. Scrape. Scrape.

But as he finally works the broken fragment from the soil, he feels like crying.

The day soon becomes as cool as the morning was, and clothes drenched, dirt entrenched in every fingernail, Sam finally calls it. He stands and straightens, observing his handiwork, considering it not as wasted time, just another step closer to finding what he needs. He prises his latest find from his pocket, spits on it, and rubs it against his shirt, inspecting the pottery shard that will join other uncovered treasures on his shelf.

"Tomorrow's the day." It has to be, he thinks, because then it will be Monday again, and a whole week will need to be endured.

But the voices plead for him to continue now, not to give up. You're so close, Sam. Riches beyond your imagination.

"I can't; I'm so tired."

You're our only hope. You need to find the key.

"I need to stop."

Just a bit longer. Think of—

"I need a poo, okay!"

"You better go and have one then, son," Mrs. Rainer's voice floats across from next door's garden. "Probably best keeping that sort of thing to yourself, though, petal."

Immediately turning red, Sam retreats under the wrought-iron archway and makes his way to the back door. The voices quieten, but he can still hear them issuing pleas between their whimpers.

"Find anything, mate?" his dad says, lifting his head from the newspaper.

Sam holds the piece of broken pottery up as he makes his way past.

"That's college paid for then."

Too tired to engage, Sam trudges up the stairs. He does his business, showers, and throws himself on the bed, eyes on Indiana on the wall to his right, whip in hand. I need a poo, words he could never imagine leaving the adventurer's lips.

"Sorry, Indy."

It was after watching Temple of Doom with his dad that he became hooked, for hours afterwards jumping from couch to couch, rolling across the carpet, offering a flick of his hand as he rose to his feet. Nobody else compares to Indiana as far as he's concerned. Lots of wannabes and try-hards, but the required level of coolness always evades.

As the voices in his head notch up, he cycles through the playlist on his phone, settling on the tried and tested theme tune for—you guessed it. He closes his eyes and imagines himself climbing mountains, crossing rivers, fighting through jungle, long-lost jewels spilling through his fingers as he flashes his best Indiana smile. But now the enemy is chasing him, machetes swinging only inches from his—

"Dinner's ready!"

He manages to duck under the first blade, but a big fella approaches from the right, cutting down the jungle, eyes hungry for the crystal skull gripped in his left hand. But he's slow, and Sam quickly side-steps to the left. Big fella comes at him again, the blade whistling above his—

"Dinner's ready, Sam!"

"I heard you the first time, Mum!" He sighs, turns off the music, and pushes himself from the bed, discarding the towel and dressing in Jeans and his favourite Indiana T-shirt. His muscles ache, his fingers sing, but he'll be back in the yard as soon as the sun rises, starting on a new patch. "Fortune and glory, kid. Fortune and glory."

Downstairs, there's no adventuring to be had, just the clink of cutlery on plates and conversation Indiana would want no part of. He shovels in his food as quickly as possible, leg tapping under the table.

"Important meeting to get to, Sam?"

"Huh?"

"Feels like I'm on the bloody Titanic, boy."

"Geoff, leave him be." Sheila reaches out for Sam's arm, but he recoils. Knowing better than to take it personally, she offers a smile and lifts the wine glass to her lips. "More potatoes?"

"I'm good, thanks, Mum."

"It's going to be a nice day tomorrow, son," Geoff says, chasing peas around his plate. "I thought we could walk around the walls and do some geocaching."

"Can't tomorrow, Dad."

Geoff offers Sheila a glance, assuring her he has things under control. "We can stop off at that burger joint you like. I'll even—"

"Not tomorrow, Dad."

"Come on, son; it will be fun."

"Uh-huh. Not tomorrow."

Feeling Sheila's foot connect with his ankle, Geoff narrows his eyebrows and turns his stare towards her. He's not ready to give up yet, words bouncing violently around his head. "You used to love exploring the ruins."

"Maybe next weekend." Sam sits back in his chair, right leg still going like the clappers and the left one not far behind. The ruins once carried some intrigue, for sure, but he's been there and done that, and the added carrot of using a phone to look for plastic boxes containing kids' grubby toys no longer carries appeal. "Can I go now?"

A frustrated sigh leaves Geoff's lips as Sheila leans in towards him, winning the battle of the eyebrows. "I guess so," he concedes.

"We can watch Indiana together later, though," Sam says, pushing his chair out.

"Maybe next weekend, son."

"K."

"That's petty, Geoff," Sheila says after hearing the creak of the fourth step. "Real petty."

"You bloody watch it with him then!"

"You know it's not my type of film."

"It's not mine anymore." Geoff begins collecting their dishes. "Getting to the point I wish the enemies would shoot on bloody target."

Back in his room, Sam stares at the crack running across his ceiling. At the right angle, it looks a bit like Indiana's whip, he thinks. "Tomorrow's the day. Tomorrow's the day." He's not sure if the mantra is to appease himself or the voices.

There's still some light out. At least another hour of digging.

"Leave me be. I'm tired."

But so many riches await.

He turns to his side. "Tomorrow." As he wraps his fingers around the pack of spoons under his pillow, more for comfort than anything else, he feels his eyelids closing and the voices beginning to fade. He tries to fight it, but not for long.

It's a seamless transition.

He's in the kitchen, one hand wrapped around the back door handle, the other clenching the packet of spoons. Taking a deep breath, he turns the knob and pulls the door inwards.

No houses, no fence. Just mud, grass, and trees.

In the absence of streetlights fizzing illusions of warmth, stark pale moonlight does its best to illuminate the nothingness. Still, vastness swallows it, and such openness provides a sense of vulnerability and a feeling that out here, Sam is the centre of nobody's universe. He exhales slowly, walking through his breath cloud, eyes on the first spoon and trying his best to summon his inner Indy.

He's tried bringing other things across—a torch, his phone, chocolate, his replica Indiana gun—but spoons are the only things that ever made it through, as if they are his connection to this hallowed ground and all its promised secrets. After all, the very first time he sank the spoon into his back garden one dull Sunday afternoon was the first time the buzz began to transition into something else, something more. And as sweat accumulated on his clothes, the stronger the frequency became, until he could make out distant but audible voices. *Others are coming for it; you have to hurry.*

That night was also the first time he had the dream, or whatever one would call this. Alone and cold in the darkness, he initially wanted nothing more than to be back in bed, running from boulders, side-stepping enemies, but all under the protection of his blankets. Even felt the trickle of warmth down his thigh when the door closed behind him for the first time. "I can't do this. Let me back in. Let me back in!" he screamed into the darkness.

And so, his obsession with Indiana Jones truly began—a means of nourishing himself with bravery and heroism. Since then, he's spent his time digging until his fingers can no longer grip the spoon or until darkness swallows the light, determined to make sure no goons make it there before him.

"We've got this, Indy."

The wind wraps around him, but adrenaline numbs everything apart from the need to find the X on the non-existent map. Catching the moon's glimmer on the back of the first spoon, he ups his pace, skin prickling at the thought of nearing the end of this adventure. And he knows he is; he just knows it. During light, voices are as clear as whispers in his ears, and there's little left of this place he's yet to conquer.

Ahead and to either side, a layer of thin mist floats hauntingly above the grass. He's heard things within it, others likely trying to get to the prize before him. He skips into a slow jog, eyes on the second spoon.

Like from a fairy tale his mum used to read him, he started placing spoons down every thirty or forty yards, knowing if he ventured out of bounds, the sequence would end, and he'd have to wait another day. So many paths, so many failed attempts, but this recent one has taken him further than he's ever been allowed to travel.

Third spoon, just beyond the trees to the right. He's almost sprinting now, drawn towards the familiar babble of the river where he guesses there'd be a school big enough for nearly five hundred kids back in the real world. Aside from the water's flow, the sound of his footfalls, and the occasional whispers from the mist and rustle of the trees, it's impossibly quiet. No birds singing their songs, no dogs barking, no other signs of life whatsoever.

The fourth spoon lays just before the small hillock ahead. He comes in fast, jumping over the mound and performing a roll, finishing with his signature wrist flick. "Eat your heart out, Indiana."

Earth is damp alongside the riverbank, his feet squelching into moistness, bitterness filling his nostrils. Wearing shoes removes his connection to the ground, though, and from the very first time he visited without them, his toes nestling into the long grass, he began picking up on it—a hum—his feet acting like a metal detector of sorts. And boy, do they sing now.

Fifth spoon. Sixth. Seventh. Eighth. Blood pulsating in his ears, involuntary shudders rattling through him; he follows the path until he gets to spoon number twenty-two, the very last one placed. He swallows hard, surveying the line of trees, knowing there's only one route left to take.

Straight ahead.

He snaps his head to the left, feeling sure he hears a rustle. But as he stands there, holding onto his breath as he has done countless times before, no enemies appear. He inhales slowly, trying to force his heart rate down. "I think it's time to ask yourself; what do you believe in?" Another quote he's been dying to use, words orated with the hope of inspiring bravery.

After counting to three, he makes his move, doubling over to avoid the sharpness of the branches, being careful not to catch his foot on the serpent-like roots twisting in and out of the soft ground.

So far, so good.

He's ventured left and right from this spot, both paths prompting the ground to open and swallow him whole, plunging him back into the real world, where only memories of this place exist. Needlessly, he crouches and places a spoon down, enjoying the softness of the earth beneath his fingers. He feels its feedback, too, the hum growing ever stronger, lighting up his nerve endings and swelling his anticipation. Sweeping the trees for any signs of movement, he continues forward, stretching his jaw to unblock his ears.

"Holy shit. Holy fucking shit."

Behind another small cluster of trees, he spies a crumbling wall.

"Can you see it, Indy? Can you see it?"

He swallows hard, ducking under more spindly branches as he reaches towards it, letting out a long exhale as his fingers wrap around solidity. He follows it around, tracing his palm across its undulating height, eyes scanning the cracked stone floor as he reminds himself to breathe.

"Indy!"

His skin fizzes at the additional connection as he crawls towards the trapdoor. Concerns of tripwires and sinking platforms melt away as he manically swipes at brown leaves, moisture in his eyes as an overwhelming feeling of pride and achievement washes over him. "I did it. I only bloody did it!" His dirt-encrusted fingernails claw at wood and metal, eventually finding the edge of the lock.

All those days spent digging, all the excuses to get out of doing things with his parents. The constant bullying at school for being different, countless names spat at the boy sitting on his own, clutching a spoon to his chest.

"I'll show them. I'll show them."

The rusty handle is too tempting not to try, but there's no give. That's okay, though; he'll return soon—tomorrow, hopefully—key in hand, ready to claim what is his. He slides a spoon from the packet and slams it onto the wood, offering a howl to the moon.

"Fortune and glory." He rolls onto his back and takes in the expanse of darkness. He smiles, which turns into a giggle, soon transitioning into a full-blown eye-watering guffaw. "I knew it. I bloody knew it!"

The buzzing—a bane of his life for as long as he can recall, but somehow, he always knew it was more than just a redundant annoyance.

Arms behind his head, he closes his eyes and breathes in the impossibly pure air.

***

It's still dark out as he wakes in his own bed. The covers are warm and soft, a complete contrast to the concrete and wood he was sprawled across only a few hours ago. Nevertheless, he swings his legs out of bed and pushes his toes into his slippers. 4.06 am reads his phone but thoughts of waiting for another school week to pass spur him on. He tiptoes down the hallway with renewed excitement, holding his breath as he passes his parents' room, finally wrapping his fingers around the banister and swinging himself down the stairs. He jumps from the fifth, performs his signature roll, and sprints to the back door.

Unlike a few hours ago, darkness brings more than whispers in the mist. Sam can hear the hum of early morning traffic from the main road. Air is no longer pure, contaminated with all the pollutants of the modern day. Beyond the garden fence, he sees the houses squashed together, dirty yellow light washing their walls.

"Let's do this."

He marches to the pile of bent metal, drops to his knees, and slides a fresh spoon from the packet. His mum asked him once, "Why spoons?" He didn't really have an answer. He thought about it later, but nothing remarkable manifested, only that it felt right.

And he's off, working at the fresh patch of ground.

Dig, Sam, dig.

"What does it look like I'm doing?"

The others are nearly here, Sam. Dig!

"But I've claimed it. They can't have it! I put a spoon there."

Sam!

"Just shut up; I'm doing it, aren't I?"

Once again, he begins humming the theme tune, but the voices refuse to dampen. It's as if he can feel warm breath against his ear.

Dig, Sam. Faster!

"Are there emeralds?"

The faster you dig, the sooner you'll know.

"Rubies?"

Yes. We have a crown for you, Sam, encrusted with them.

"Will you tell me who you are now?"

We're your spiritual guides, Sam, leading you to your destiny.

Feedback vibrates through his arm, his fingers already feeling like someone else's as he scrapes, scrapes, scrapes. "Not this bit." He moves two inches to the right and starts again. The knowledge of the key being further down than he could ever dig haunts him, or worse still, that there's no key at all, that his mind is simply fabricating his escape from a world of disappointment and pain. But those thoughts are usually fleeting, drowned out by sparkling jewels and the look on the faces of his audience.

He grits his teeth and plunges the spoon into the top layer. Again and again, he brings it down until the buckling metal becomes redundant and tossed onto the ever-growing pile. He slides a fresh one from the packet and repeats. Hours pass, the first light of morning showing itself as he moves onto his sixth hole and goes through the motions.

Two inches down, the spoon connects with something.

He's been here before, though, disappointment bound. Yet as he tries to slow his breathing down, something feels different, the air charged like just before a storm, and the ground feeding him energy with as much urgency as the voices in his ear.

Dig, Sam! Dig! Dig! Dig!

And as he scrapes another layer of earth across with a trembling hand, he can hardly believe his eyes. "Shit on a stick. Shit on a stick."

He works some more of the earth free. "Shit on a motherfucking stick." It's a word that's never made it from his mind to his lips before, and one his mum would be upset to hear him say—I'm not mad, just disappointed—but he's just uncovered a key to long lost treasures, so she can kiss his ass as far as he's concerned.

He stares at it, taking it in—heavy-looking, dull against the soil, and likely easy to miss using anything larger than a spoon, especially under the half-moonlight. Felt right.

"I did it."

The rest of his body begins to tremble. He blinks hard, making sure it's real. All this time, all those early mornings and late evenings, all those spoons wrecked.

"I found it."

Come, Sam. Your treasure awaits.

"I found it. By myself!"

Sam, the others are on their way.

"But I have the key, not them."

It might not be the only one, Sam.

And the thought prompts him to scoop the key from the soil and clutch it to his heart. It's as heavy as it looks, which only emphasises its importance. It might not be the only one. They might be right, he considers. There are three keys to this house, one for each of them. "No way. It's my fucking treasure!" As the bedroom light comes on next door, he ducks under cover of darkness and shimmies along the side of the house.

Hurry, Sam.

"I am!"

Heart thumping, he tiptoes across the kitchen floor and up the stairs, skipping over the fourth and almost falling up the second half. Key still clutched tightly to his chest; he dances gingerly across the hallway to his bedroom, squeezing through the gap in his door and sliding under the covers, finally releasing a loud exhale, and screwing his eyes shut tight.

This is the easy bit, Sam; just close your eyes and sleep.

"I'm trying." But blood pulsates in his ears, and his legs are going like the clappers.

Concentrate, Sam. It's all here waiting for you.

He starts doing maths problems in his head, which usually helps him along. If that fails, he tries to recount his collection of console games, sorting them into alphabetical order. There's always plan C, but he read somewhere that it can fall off if you do it too much.

Are you nearly asleep, Sam?

"Look, just fuck off and let me be, will you." He turns to his side, nestling into the softness of the pillow. "It's too much pressure."

But even as the voices abate, that other plane only seems to grow more distant. His body is alive, singing, lighting up with patches of hyperactive nerve endings. Like an itch he cannot scratch, his dirty and chewed fingernails offer only temporary relief, moving the army of invisible ants from one section to the next. He turns over, eyes on Indiana, suddenly convinced someone will beat him to the punch. He checks his phone: 6.35 am. Time is running out, his parents insisting he's always out of his pit before 9 am on a weekend. "What would you do, Indy?" And as if the man himself responds, the idea manifests in his head.

After dragging his weary body from the bed, he tiptoes to the bathroom. He knows where she keeps them—in the small silver bucket on the top shelf with her lady things. Parents give kids too much trust, he thinks. Hardly an inch of the house he's not been through with a fine-tooth comb, on the hunt for Christmas, Birthday presents, and whatnot. And bearing in mind, he has no real friends; there isn't much else for a kid to do all day. He's seen some things he shouldn't have, too, the kind he wished he could unsee.

One tablet just before bed.

He empties two from the bottle and fills the plastic cup half full of water. His mum started taking them just after her sister died of cancer. He often watched from his parent's bedroom door, too scared to approach, his mum's face swollen with tears, his dad doing his best to console her. It was a tough period, but she's better now, at least most of the time. He swallows the two small tablets, half-expecting to pass out there and then.

By the time he gets between the sheets, the bed is cold again. He takes a deep breath, wraps his fingers around the metal key, and begins counting down from ten. Nothing. He tries again, counting more slowly, but frustration sets in as he reaches zero, even after repeating and going down in halves. He turns his attention to the crack in the ceiling, slowly following its path from the coving to the—

***

A Molotov cocktail of fear, excitement, and anticipation explode in his mind as he pulls the door towards him. Inhale. Exhale. He can feel the weight of the key in his left hand but uncoils his fingers anyway just to make sure.

"Fortune and glory."

As the unpolluted breeze blows across, bringing only the scent of moss and dead leaves, Sam begins the short journey for what he knows will be the last time. Spoon after spoon, he does his best to stay calm, taking deep breaths, thoughts turning to what he'll spend his fortune on. He knows he'll have to give his parents some but having no friends will surely come in handy for once.

Squeezing down on the key, he snaps his head towards a patch of mist to his left. Whispering? His mind playing tricks? Regardless, he ups his pace, eyes on the next spoon as he jogs alongside the riverbank. Spoon to spoon; he senses the finality, the end scene not far away.

He takes another deep breath and drops his pace to a march as he enters the first line of trees. "This is it, Indy." He ducks under branches, steps over the contorted limbs, and readies himself as best he can for what lies ahead.

There it is—the wall.

He marches towards it, head snapping left and right, but there's no sign of anyone else, and the spoon rests undisturbed atop the wooden trapdoor. Stomach churning, blood whooshing in his ears, he drops to his hands and knees. "Please work. Please work." He takes one last look around and enters the key into the hole, skin prickling as the lock offers a satisfying click.

"Shit on a stick."

Fingers coiled around the handle, veins popping in his skinny arms; he heaves at the door, managing to get it halfway and letting momentum do the rest. It slams hard against the concrete, and he holds his breath, scanning the trees, but still, no surprises.

"Shit on a stick. Shit on a stick. Shit on a stick."

Concrete steps lead down into uninviting darkness, but he's come this far and isn't about to back out. "Hello?" Using the hole's edge, he lowers himself onto the first step, waiting for the wave of dizziness to pass before moving to the second. "Is anyone here?" His eyes slowly begin to adjust, the slither of moonlight assisting, but only after taking two further steps can he make out the concrete floor beneath and the two sets of shackles on the far wall. "Hello?"

There's a sudden urge to run, take himself out of bounds and back to predictable tedium, but, hair on the back of his neck prickling and stomach knotting, he continues his descent, knowing regret would be waiting at home, ready to bite him on the ass and then swallow him whole. "Hello?" he says as his foot finally finds the floor.

Hello Sam.

He snaps his head towards the voices, but moonlight falls short of the corner recess.

Have you come for your treasure?

Still resisting the urge to run, he shifts his weight onto his right foot in preparation. The place smells off to him, more than just damp, earthy. Something not right, something—

It's right here, Sam.

He swallows hard, opening his mouth to speak but finding no words.

Don't be scared.

But he's fucking terrified. He swallows again, not a drop of saliva in his mouth. "Where is it?" he manages to croak.

Come closer, and we'll show you. Giggling follows, but he continues shuffling forward, impossibly cold air wrapping around him. "I don't know about this anymore."

But your crown awaits, Sam.

He freezes, arching his neck, willing the darkness to dissipate. "I think I—" Iciness grips around his wrist, yanking him forward. He lets out a high-pitched scream, reaching his hands to avoid crashing into the wall as childish laughter emerges from behind, the kind he's heard on the playground many times before.

King Sam! King Sam! King Sam!

He slowly turns to face his taunters, not an ounce of bravado left in his twelve-year-old body. Through the rectangular hole, the trespassing moon spotlights two identical girls holding hands, broad smiles breaking across pale and dirty faces, brittle hair laying over spindly shoulders. They're dressed in tattered rags and look as far from royalty as one could imagine. Sam backs up against the wall, pinching at his thigh to try and wake himself up. "Who—who are you, and where's my treasure?"

They raise a hand to their lips in unison, tittering as they step towards him. Their movement is ethereal, legs going through the motions, but their footfalls are silent. "We've been waiting so long to meet you, Sam."

Sam squeezes tighter on his flesh, but he knows this isn't how it works. "I want to go home."

Their laughter ceases, their grins flatten. "Do you know how long we've been down here, Sam?"

"I don't want to know. I just want to go home." He grinds himself against the wall as though trying to push through. "You can keep the treasure."

"Oh, silly Sam. There's nothing here but the souls of the damned."

He glances towards the rectangular hole, preparing to make a run for it, unsure if his legs will carry him.

"We've been reaching out for decades, but you're the only one who ever heard us."

"I don't understand." He feels his way along the wall, getting ready to push off.

"They called us witches, demons, put us in those shackles, left us to rot." The girls continue their approach, hands locked together and swinging back and forth. "It was him that turned us in, that devil in sheep's clothing, wanted all the evil to himself."

"What has this got to—" Mouth agape he watches the twins' hair rise towards the ceiling and begin dancing in the air, twitching like kite strings. They look angry, lips curled, hands clasped and swaying back and forth even more vigorously.

"He made a special key," they continue, "a cursed one that would cast our souls away in limbo and lock our lips together. If it weren't for being able to hear each other's thoughts, we'd have had nothing for company bar the whisper of demons carrying on the mist—others like us, trapped by him."

"But I could hear you?"

"That's because you're special, too, Sam."

"You just needed the key to escape, didn't you?" He swallows hard, chewing on the inside of his lip. Now or never. Now or never. "There never was any treasure, was there?"

"We knew it was close, could sense the malignance, smell it on what breeze wafted through the gaps, but that didn't help us. You did, though, Sam."

"I need to go home now."

"Oh, Sam, but you unlocked the curse." A smile creeps across their faces, not evil, not warm. "You're different, like us. And to feel its energy, to be able to hear our thoughts from another plane; we belong together. This is our destiny."

"Mum's cooking pancakes for breakfast."

"Don't worry, Sam, we'll be there."

He finally makes his run, getting two decent strides in before hair as dry as hay wraps around his neck, jerking him to a halt. Eyes wide and bulging, he begins pulling at the long strands, wincing as his fingers glide across—dampness? He can feel it on his neck, a cold clamminess slithering, tightening around his skin. No longer brittle threads, the twins' hair takes the form of thin serpents, coiling, writhing, hissing, reeling him in towards them as they await with open arms. He leans back, crumpled face turned away as he lashes out blindly. Snakes! Why did it have to be snakes?

"It will all be over soon, Sam. Try not to resist."

"Please, don't do this," he rasps.

"It's okay, Sam." They each grab a hand and bring him towards them, their touch impossibly cold, their eyes hungry for freedom. "We feel the anger within you, Sam. All the bullying, all the talking behind your back. You're not alone anymore."

As the serpents coil tighter still, Sam feels like his head might explode. The twins watch him unempathetically, squeezing down on his hands as he tries to snatch himself free, only a garbled croak emerging from his lips.

"Stop fighting it, Sam."

Blackness hovers threateningly on the outside of his vision, the death tide waiting to come in. Pain intensifies, his fingers slipping and sliding across wet scaly skin. He thinks of his mum calling to his room that breakfast is ready. He thinks of how mean he was to Harvey the day before. He thinks he will surely die.

The twins begin to laugh again, but this is no titter; this is a menacing cackle full of the threat to make up for time lost. Under the pale moonlight, rasping and wheezing, Sam watches the twins' skin become even more translucent until it's as thin as the mist above ground.

Until it is mist.

He doubles over, on the edge of oblivion, hungrily sucking in air, hands at his throat. There's no sign of the girls or the serpent, but as soon as he swallows, he tastes the badness and feels it working its way through his body, spreading through his mind like mould.

"You're not alone anymore, Sam."

The voice is his, but the words aren't.

What is happening?

Laughter leaves his lips while his head fills with thoughts—so many bad ones—violent images of revenge against humanity. And him, the one who locked them away, the one who likely still walks with the mortals.

"It's time, Sam."

Shackled without water or food, left to rot, their souls trapped for countless decades, he feels their anger boiling his blood.

"We'll show them, Sam. We'll show them."

He's in there somewhere, but he's not in control, just a passenger watching his feet climb the steps into the moonlight.

One by one, they follow the spoons to the open back door of Sam's house.

No fortune, no glory.

GOLDEN CHILD

England, Late October 1986

He's got him; he's sure of it—defeat in his eyes. "You know you want to, Smithy. Come on."

"I just don't know, Charlie. It's a good deal, but—"

"Do it then. Don't think about it. Thinking's for broken-hearted."

Smithy shakes his head and creases his forehead. "Huh?"

"Never mind." It seemed like a good play at the time, a line from one of his mum's favourite songs, but he needs to get the boy nodding, not shaking.

Josh looks at his watch again. They've been at it for nearly fifty minutes and don't seem any closer. "Come on, guys, I've got to get home for tea."

"Shut it, Josh," Charlie snaps. "We're negotiating."

"Jeez, alright." Josh buries his chin into his neck. "They're only stickers."

Charlie readies himself to unleash at his friend but thinks better of it. "You're right. You're absolutely right, Josh. See, Smithy, they're only stickers. And look, you're getting six of mine for one of yours." He holds the glossy cards up like ten-pound notes and wafts them in his face. "Just think how much closer you'll be to filling the book."

"Yeah, but mine's silver," Smithy says, shifting his glance to his own watch.

"Don't mean squat. There are as many out there as there are of the others; it's just a myth." Too much, damn it! His dad said it's okay to skew the truth but never offer an outright lie, and he sold forty cars last month, so he knows what he's talking about.

Smithy offers another shake of his head. "Mum's doing lasagne for tea. I best be getting home."

"She can fucking wait!"

Both Smithy and Josh snap their head towards Charlie, and an awkward silence blankets the corner of the small playground.

Calm, Charlie, Calm. "Smithy, this is just about you and me. The planets have aligned so that we can do this deal."

"I don't know, Charlie."

"Fuck's sake," Josh mutters.

"I'm only asking for Tunnel Stalker."

"It's a silver, though."

Charlie feels the deal slipping away. It's time to go for broke, pull out all the stops. No more Mister Nice Guy. "Smithy, how are you ever going to get through life without making a decision?"

The kid shrugs.

"Smithy, this is a big moment. A coming-of-age thing. And to tell you the truth, you're fucking it up."

Josh does a one-eighty and kicks a tuft of grass, starting to feel bad for the kid.

"Did you decide what to have for breakfast this morning?" Charlies says, leaning in.

Smithy nods.

"Did you decide where you'd sit on the school bus this morning?"

Smithy nods again.

"Did you decide what underwear you'd wear today?"

Smithy shrugs.

"Oh, Jesus." Charlie reaches a hand to the kid's shoulder. "Two out of three ain't bad, but three out of four sounds better. What do you say, kid?"

"I'll sleep on it, Charlie. Talk to me tomorrow."

"Tomorrow? Tomorrow the planets fall out of the sky, Smithy. Tomorrow might never come. Tomorrow is—"

"Nearly here," Josh says but regrets it instantly as he feels the sting against his neck. The acorn lands near his feet, and he boots it into the damp grass.

"Tomorrow, Charlie." Smithy gets up and slips the precious silver card back into the front sleeve of his album. "I've got to go."

"Alright, fuck off, you prick." He watches the kid make his way to the other side of the playground; album carefully tucked under his right arm. "Other people want these, though. You'll live to regret this, Smithy!"

"Mark my words," Josh mumbles under his breath. "Thought you had him, there, Charlie. Maybe you're losing your touch."

"That was your fucking fault," Charlie says, pushing himself up from the gravel and giving his pants an angry brush down.

"How do you make that out?"

"I've got to get home for tea," Charlie mimics in a less than favourable voice. "Do you think Richard Branson ever said that? Sorry, guys, I've got to put this billion-dollar deal on ice because my chips are burning?"

"I guess not, Charlie, but I'm sure as shit Richard Branson picks out his own underwear."

"Good point." He slides the cards carefully back into the little plastic wallet and into the album's inside sleeve. "God damn it! Only three more, and the book is full."

The pair begin making their way across the field towards Spencer Road, breathing in the scent of earthy mud and thinking about all the useless ways they can fill their evening.

"Johnno only needs two silvers. I can't let him beat me, Josh."

"Man, you're obsessed. I've not seen you this excitable since Amy Winters asked to stroke your dog."

"Yeah. My hot dog."

They laugh until they have tears in their eyes, setting each other off again as they approach composure, Charlie even momentarily forgetting about the two silvers and gold. Only the sight of Richard Hoggins and crew near the corner shop throws a heavy blanket on their fire.

"Shit!" Charlie stops dead, hoping they haven't seen him already.

"Why does he hate you?"

"He hates everyone, just me that little bit more." Charlie edges away, taking cover behind a large oak and driving his back against the bark. "I can't go that way, Josh. No way. If he gets hold of my stickers!"

"Mate, I have to get back. I'm already on a warning."

"If he asks, tell him I'm already at home, yeah? Shit! I knew it was a bad idea bringing them with me."

"Of course, Charlie. That's a hell of a long way round, though, isn't it?"

"Just go, Josh! From where they're standing, you're talking to a tree."

"Okay, okay. It's cool. See you tomorrow, yeah?"

"Yeah, just go."

Charlie gives it a few seconds before sticking his head out to see Josh approaching the road, head down, not running, but as good as. He hears one of the crew, possibly Richard himself, holler something, but traffic swallows any further exchange. For what seems like an eternity, he waits for them to leave, praying he won't need to go through 'Thorny Passage,' under the old railway line tunnel, and finally, through the field with the scarecrow and decrepit barn. Those types of experiences are for sharing, a ritual that conjures brave-talking but also elevated heart rates and skin that crawls.

But he's kidding himself. Those kids have nowhere to go, never will.

You've got this, Charlie. He scoots behind the cover of the next tree. "Hate you, Smithy." Another peek, but they're like smoking statues. He contemplates just waiting it out, but on the occasions when his dad forces him to help with food shopping, he's seen them there well past seven.

Shit on a stick.

His stomach stirs as he takes in a few breaths of earthiness mixed with cooking food. He'll be at least thirty minutes late; no silver card and a whole heap of shit from his parents.

Three.

Two.

One.

The marshy ground gives underneath as he makes his run, backpack swinging wildly behind, sticker album tucked tightly under his right arm. He glances to the right, but so far, so good. Thorny Passage awaits only thirty yards ahead, but if they see him now, there's a good chance they'll follow, and that'll take things up a notch. Come on! Thoughts of the upcoming ordeal plague his mind, so he begins envisaging the blank spaces in his album to counteract. Tunnel Stalker, Mole Man, and Swamp Thing are all that stand between him and notoriety among his peers.

Tunnel Stalker. Fucking Tunnel Stalker. It had to be, didn't it!

Another glance to his right shows the crew is none the wiser. He slows his pace to a jog as he approaches the gravelly path, spiky tendrils like barbed-wire fencing looming on the other side, along with the faded poster of the missing kid attached to the lamp post. He takes cover, turning to his side, ready to shimmy through.

Please leave. Please leave.

A last hopeful glance across, but realisation dawns that he has no choice. Trying to avoid eye contact with the poor kid's face on the poster, he shakes off the backpack, unzips it, and carefully slides the album in. Okay. Okay. Holding the pack tight to his chest, he breathes in and begins to side-step, screwing his face up as thorns start pulling at his clothes and skin. A distant holler snaps his head around, and his stomach drops.

Blood pounds in his ears as he holds his breath—but no voices. He carries on, shrugging off the spiky attackers and pulling the pack even tighter to his chest.

Fucking Smithy. Fucking Josh!

He misses his best friend already, though, each step taking him further into the bowels of the thorny beast. Ducking and weaving as best he can, the prickly vines seem intent on claiming him, and frustration finally sets in as his right foot gets tangled, quickly turning to pressure behind his eyes as he rips it away, catching the side of his cheek with a good one. He traces the wound with the index finger of his right hand and inspects the magnificent red against his paleness. Finally, bringing it to his lips, he finds himself wondering if he even took the right opening; if one day, someone might stumble upon his remains, thorny tendrils emerging from the eyeholes of his skull.

Fucking hell, Charlie, get a grip.

But he remains on the verge of tears until, through a gap in the thorns, he catches sight of the embankment and the rusty roof of the old makeshift station.

The last of the vines latches onto his jumper, but he tears away easily and throws the backpack across his shoulders, ready for stage two, the climb. He takes a breath and begins his ascent, tufts of wet grass and the occasional clump of damp brown leaves making for a challenging scramble, but momentum carries him forward, that and the urgency to get home. Finally, at the top, he affords himself a few gulps of leafy air.

No going back now, Charlie.

He thinks about form class on Thursday morning and how well his story of bravery will go down; how he took the shady route home just for the hell of it. A gust of cool wind highlights the evidence on his face and serves as a prompt for him to stop crapping and get cracking. Tunnel next.

"Okay, let's do this."

He lowers himself to the grassy decline, extends his toes, and digs his heels into the ground, shuffling his bum across a few inches at a time. It's a perfect system until his palm finds a semi-crusty pile of white dog shit hiding in a flurry of tall grass. He can hear Josh's laughter in his head. "What are the chances?" he would say, or something along those lines.

There's a bittersweet feeling as Charlie wipes his hand on the grass. Dog poo. Dogs. He thinks about their German Shepherd, Basil, waiting patiently at the window for his return.

Easing himself down the rest of the hill, he notes how ominous the tunnel looks in the distance. Strangely longer, too, as if it's grown recently, along with the vegetation.

No going back.

He surveys the disused railway line. A case of nature meets humans, and nature is winning. Long grasses and vines work through gravel and spill over the rusty frames of the tracks, even beginning to swallow the brickwork of the tunnel ahead.

So damned dark in there.

He sets off, the urge to cry gone, but the hairs on his neck bristling their warning.

The low sun causes him to squint on the approach, but he still notices the abundance of rabbits scampering and fleeing back to their homes. Stranger danger. He raises an arm as the glare worsens, but not before he catches sight of something glimmering from the tunnel's depths. Gone just as quick, though.

What was that?

Arching his neck, he searches again but only finds fluffy grey floaters as the sun's rays hit him full on. Another chilly gust blows across as he squelches at his eyes with the ball of his right hand. Temperature's dropping. Thoughts of being out here without sunlight spur him back into action, and he begins a jog towards the tunnel's opening.

The plan is to sprint right through. Not overly complex, but at least it's a plan. He guesses he can do it in twenty seconds tops. Twenty seconds, Charlie; that's nothing. He reaches an arm out towards the brick and performs a futile series of stretches, noting the graffiti scrawled across the entrance.

For a good time, call Charlie Davenport's mum.

"That fucker!" He guesses the handiwork of Richard and his minions. Wrong number. Still. That fucker.

Mid-limber, it catches his eye again—something on the floor, just on the border of where dark meets light. He'll stick to the right, away from oblivion.

Three. A couple of deep breaths of earthy dampness mixed with a tinge of stale urine.

Two. He yanks a leg behind his back, just like on his mum's aerobic videos.

One. Oh shit!

And he's off, arms and legs going like the clappers and as close to the tunnel wall as he can get without being part of it. Coldness wraps around him, and the putrid cocktail on entry fades to something much worse, something he'll try and forget as soon as light washes over him. He hears gravel crunching under his shoes but can't feel his legs. Darkness seems to be spilling towards him from the sides with each step, and what the fuck was that? He snaps his head to the left, but only a dark void awaits. Cold air stings his lungs as his arms swing by his side, more of a desperate clawing at the air than good form as if trying to grab onto an invisible rope.

Another glimmer.

No! No way!

He draws closer, a second wind, teeth digging into his lip, heart feeling dangerously close to exploding.

There's just no way.

But it's not a trick of the light, after all.

A fucking silver!

Over the pounding blood in his ears and the clunk of steel as he dances across one of the rails, he thinks he hears a noise from behind, but a glance over his shoulder only finds unlit recesses. He snaps his head back around, eyes on the prize but still unable to make it out. Preparing for collection, he stoops, knowing the odds are—

Tunnel Stalker!

Long and gangly limbs, skin almost translucent against contrastingly stringy black hair and menacing eyes, he knows the creature off by heart. He's envisaged the card so many times as if he could somehow conjure it from thin air. With fingers stretched out, he lowers his arm to the ground, grimacing as he catches the sharpness of gravel but not recoiling.

And—strike!

His fingers catch the edge, but he fumbles it, only managing to flick it over.

Shit!

He turns sharply, pushing his right foot against the semi-exposed wood.

Was that gravel crunching?

Something moves within, too, a shadow in a shadow. He saw it; he's sure of it.

Your imagination, Charlie. Suck it up.

There's an expelling of air as if someone is—breathing.

It's just in your head, Charlie!

He wants to turn and sprint for the light but knows he'll burst with regret when he gets home. A silver! Only two more after that. Before he can talk himself out of it, he thrusts himself into darkness and swoops in again, focusing on the card and nothing else, ignoring the sounds that aren't really there as he's the only one in the goddamned tunnel.

Gravel crunches. Something breathes.

It's you, Charlie, you idiot!

His fingers meet glossiness and clamp down like a crocodile's bite.

Another rasp. More grinding gravel.

With a garbled war cry, he makes his run, almost toppling over, but momentum and sheer will somehow keep him up. He hears someone calling his name from behind, the voice raspy, rattly, the stuff of nightmares. Charlie Davenport. The feeling in his legs is back, but they only scream at him to stop as his feet fall heavier with each step. So close, he can almost feel the sunlight on his face.

It's in my head. It's in my head.

What about the breathing? And you saw something move?

A rat!

Must be a big fucker.

Light falls golden ahead, and it's a heavenly sight. Home stretch! Gritting his teeth, he sprints for his life, all technique out the window, limbs jerking like a marionette on speed.

In my head!

Gravel crunches. Something hot falls across his neck.

Mum's doing fish for tea.

He glances over his shoulder before letting himself crease over, sucking in urgent mouthfuls of freshness no longer tainted by—in my head—bad things. The tears are a surprise, but he lets them flow. After all, he's pretty sure nobody's watching.

Wisps of breath pepper the air as he shuffles off the backpack and flops to the damp grasses of the embankment. He made it through the tunnel, but its mouth looks no less foreboding. Made it, though! Light dances across the sticker as he holds his reward out in front. He angles it left and right, lending animation to the emaciated form of the Tunnel Stalker. The voice plays again in his head, Charlie Davenport, and he lets out an involuntary shudder. He pictures Josh's face, the captivated look in his best friend's eyes as he runs through his account of events. Maybe he'll believe him. Maybe he won't. But the sticker sure as hell didn't drop from the sky.

He takes the album from the pack and begins flicking through the pages, knowing where he'll find the blank space waiting. It feels like a big moment, far more significant than the placement of a card from a purchased pack. He earned this one. Put his life on the line.

Well, it sounds good in his head.

Page seventy-six.

He carefully peels off the back layer, inhaling the pungent but gloriously familiar adhesive, and with a shaking hand, brings the silver trophy towards the page. The environment is usually much more controlled for the procedure, and he equates it to surgery—one wrong move, and there's no going back. But luck is on his side today, and it's a perfect placement.

Two to go.

Conscious of time, he slips the album into his pack and gets to his feet, taking one last prideful look at the conquered tunnel. He gives it the middle finger and turns, beginning his trudge towards scarecrow field, the cool breeze accentuating his now damp behind, prompting a quickening of pace.

There's undeniable trepidation of what lies ahead, but he's a tunnel beater and has a trophy to prove it. His legs feel springy again, and his heart rate begins to settle close to normal.

In my head.

A gust of iciness bites at his skin, and he buries his chin into his neck and folds his arms. The further he gets away from the tunnel, the more his mind wanders back to everyday things like being late home for tea, maths homework, Amy Winters, and the fact Johnno still has the edge, only needing two silvers. It's a long wait until pocket money day on Sunday, too. He can already see the kid's smug face as he parades around the school. "Look but don't touch." It will mean nothing then. All the deals, the extra homework, washing neighbourhood cars, watching others chew on impossibly colourful candy. And the goddamned tunnel. All for nothing!

He lifts his head to see a speck of a bird resting on top of the fence in the distance, just visible over the slight rise. On the other side of it, he knows the tracks veer off to the left, leading their way to where the next station used to stand. Part of the golf course now where his dad sometimes plays.

Halfway home, Charlie!

He ups his tempo as the wind wraps around him. It's getting cold, and he's not dressed for it, his thin jumper offering little protection, and the arse of his half-mast pants wet through. His nose feels like ice as he wipes a string of mucus away. Alternating between a march and a jog, he soon nears the edge of the field, and in the distance, sees the scarecrow's chequered black and yellow shirt flapping in the breeze, and behind it, the barn he and Josh joked was full of missing children.

His feet finally leave the gravel and begin treading silently on grass that spills through the bottom of the rickety fence. He coils his fingers around the soft wood, surveying the path ahead, squinting into the low light that catches the moisture on the grass. A beautiful sight if not for the—fucking scarecrow. He plans his route carefully, eyes carving their way down the right side of the field past the ominous figure and back to the centre, away from the pools of brown and that godawful barn.

Halfway, Charlie.

The fence gives a little as he straddles it, but he safely drops to the other side, shoes sinking into softness. With a cursory shuffle of his backpack, he sets off, staying close to the fence and trying to avoid the boggier patches that become more abundant with every step. He picks his spots, pointing his toes like a ballerina one minute and taking fairy steps the next, eyes occasionally darting towards the hay-filled fucker with gravel for eyes.

Paranoia, on this occasion, pays.

Hardly able to believe it, he watches it lift against a small rise of grass as another blast of cutting wind rears up. He sees flashing black and yellow from peripheral vision, but his stare remains firmly fixed on the patch of ground twenty yards to his left and just short of a sizable puddle of brown. The wind cuts out, and the card falls back, silver side up. Swamp Thing. Momentarily, he can't move; he just stands there, mouth open, transfixed by the plant-based entity framed in glorious silver.

He tests the ground ahead. Soft, but no worse than the path trodden so far. Already lowering himself to the ground in preparation, he edges forward again. Nobody's going to believe me. He takes two steps, moving stealthily like a big cat towards its prey, adrenaline coursing through his veins. Just one more card after this. His stomach growls. Fear, excitement, hunger, in a perfect storm.

Johnno's face will be a picture.

Nearly within reach, he lets his foot come down, but the ground makes a squelching sound. He tries a different patch, but this time, the brown liquid threatens to spill into his shoe. Shit! "Just got to rip the bandage off," as his mum says. The thought fills him with sadness and a need to be home. Fish for tea. He readies himself, slapping his thighs as if to wake up his legs, and as another gust of wind peters out, he makes his move, scrambling forward, grimacing as cold and dirty water finds its way into his shoe. His heavy legs scream at him as he trudges into the murk, up to his ankles now. Left leg forward, and it plunges deep. Right leg forward, and a high-pitched squeal leaves his lips as cold and dirty water settles just below his kneecap.

Fuck! Fuck! Fuck!

He sees a bubble appear on the surface of the puddle ahead.

Desperately, he tries to unplug his left leg, but it's—stuck. He throws himself forward, fingers stretched out towards the sticker, but just as they brush against its edge, the wind whistles around him, sending shirttails flapping and the silver card lifting.

The sight of another bubble replacing the last sends him into a frenzy, clawing and pushing at the soft ground, brown water splashing either side. Come on! Come on! He manages to rip his left leg free, and he takes the opportunity to reach for the card in the dying gust, continuing his earthworm squirms.

Yes!

Another bubble emerges on the brown surface, and—

Something has him. Something's latched onto his right foot.

Imagination again, Charlie.

As his left leg slides redundantly behind in a futile effort to get traction, his hands slop against mud. A ripple in the water sparks even more aggressive struggling, but it's still locked tight. Something's holding it; that's why Charlie. He fumbles at the straps of the backpack and swings it to the right, launching his upper half onto it and trying to wiggle loose. Another bubble replaces the last, far too quickly for his liking. He closes his eyes and envisages his leg coming free, and—holy shit, it's working! Thrashing his upper body left to right against marshy ground, he continues to inch forward, picturing himself running across the field to the safety of Anderson Road, waking up in a warm bed to the smell of pancakes, only needing one more sticker.

He's out, shoeless, but he's out!

Launching his backpack ahead of him, a little further each time, he uses it to drag himself as far away from the puddle as possible. It's slow progress, but it's better than having limbs exposed underground.

Finally, as he nears his visible footprints, exhausted and covered head to toe in mud but silver card spotless between his teeth, he scrambles desperately to his feet and begins his run down the right side of the field, legs leaden but still putting up one hell of a fight. He throws his backpack across his shoulders and sniffs back a string of snot that threatens to tarnish his trophy.

Feet still squelching but sinking a little less each step, he focuses on a small patch of grass ahead but well short of the scary barn. Even as he notices movement to his left, probably the wind, he doesn't let himself turn. Even as he hears something akin to splashing, likely my own damned feet, he keeps his gaze fixed on the circle of grass and his arms pumping. Even as he hears the watery rasp of his name, Charlie Davenport, he doesn't succumb to the temptation for a nervous peek. He runs for his life, doing it justice until his body finally gives up, and he doubles over, chugging on cold air and almost vomiting in the process.

In my head

In my head.

In my stupid fucking head.

In almost the dead centre of the field, standing in his nominated safe zone, chest heaving, and the silver card still between his teeth, Charlie turns back towards the large brown puddle to see nothing but his dirt-covered shoe sitting at the edge of its rim.

What the fuck? There's no way; there's just no way.

But he considers that in all the chaos, he just might not have seen it come out.

He snaps the card from his mouth, lips aching from pinching around the card's glossiness, filled with relief as he's unable to find even a single tooth mark. To be sure, he lifts it to the evening rays, but the blurry white spotlight only offers a bulky mass of green vegetation and black holes for eyes that offer only emptiness.

The watery gargle of his name, the splashing, the shoe near the puddle's rim, all in his head?

Charlie Davenport.

His body offers an exaggerated shudder above and beyond the persistent shivering, and he snaps his head towards the puddle. Back to the barn. The puddle. The barn. The puddle.

Get a grip, Charlie!

He's beyond cold. Clothes heavy with dirt, too. But he can't wait for a second longer.

As the grasses give once more to the blast of wind, Charlie presses his palm against the ground of his little haven, and satisfied he's not going to be sucked arse-first into it, he takes a seat and unzips his pack. Another sweep of the field, and another, another, and he finally opens the book.

Page thirty-two; he knows it off by heart. And the ritual takes place—unpeel, sniff, position, place.

Swamp Thing. Conquered.

He lets out a groan as he pushes himself to his feet, zipping the album back into his pack. Every part of him aches, and the chill is to his bones, not helped by the ever-increasing wind. But two fucking silvers!

One last obstacle. The one with the missing kids chained up inside.

It crosses his mind to run, but his legs have other ideas, and he decides to save his energy for when he draws level with the barn. Besides, no danger here. All in your mind, Charlie. He settles to a pace just above normal, his feet finding more solid ground, and as far as he can see, the path getting even clearer ahead. Twenty minutes or so, and he'll be home. Late for tea, and inevitably there'll be a scolding, but that's just fine; he'll take it.

One more card. Johnno's face will melt.

As the wind cuts across again, he can hardly feel his fingers, almost translucently white as he holds them out in front. He imagines holding them in front of the fire and that slightly uncomfortable but welcome tingling as they—

Shit on a stick!

Sure that his eyes are playing tricks, he follows it to the ground because there's just no way. Even with his previous finds, even as the card lands on the tuft of grass face side up, and even as the last of the light shimmers across the brown hairs, he can't bring himself to believe there are only twenty yards between him and Mole Man.

He's in the classroom, people climbing over each other to see. Oohs and aahs, and pats on the back and high-fives. Amy Winters with a twinkle in her eye. And in comes Johnno, his smile fading to a grimace as realisation dawns.

Finally, he exhales and begins his approach, skin crawling with excitement, all thoughts of children in the barn fading. Fifteen yards away, the wind gets up again, but the card lifts only slightly. His stomach growls, but he'll be home soon, eating fish and throwing Basil the scraps.

The sound of a branch snapping underfoot catches him off guard, but the gold shimmer has him like a tractor beam, and it's only ten yards from his grasp. His skin prickles as he imagines placing the final sticker in the album and being the envy of the school. He even starts running through a small speech in his head, but just as he gets to the part about the bubbling puddle, the ground begins to give.

Shhiiiiiiiiiiiiiiiiiiiiiitt.

As pain explodes in his right leg, he lets out a pained squeal and crumples to his side, nursing his ankle. Teary eyes fall across the broken branches and tufts of grass that served as his trap, Mole Man resting on top, just slightly out of reach.

From deeper within the darkness, Charlie hears breathing, and—a squeal?

In your mind, Charlie.

But this time, he doesn't buy his own bullshit.

He gets to his elbows and pushes himself backwards, thrusting his legs alternately against the ground. Dim light falls through the opening above, but the dark tunnel ahead swallows most of it.

More breathing.

With eyes on the solitary star above, he drives back into the wall of mud, offering his cards to the Gods in return for his safe passage. It must be nearly ten feet back to the surface, and no way could he climb back up, even if he wasn't already exhausted and sporting a twisted ankle.

"Help!"

His voice is weak, and besides, there's nobody up there.

"Help!"

Something's coming.

Another high-pitched screech emerges from the depths. The sound of something scraping, too.

"Please, help!"

He peers into the tunnel, warmth spreading across his thigh as he catches sight of the approaching silhouette, a huge lumbering mass of darkness, the top of its head almost trailing across the ceiling.

"Mum's doing fish for tea."

He snaps his stare towards the star and offers a final prayer but only gets another squeal for his efforts.

It finally comes into view, claws as sharp as knives carving lines in the muddy wall to its right, long snout twitching at the air in front. Short dark fur covers most of the body that stands at least seven feet tall. It has no nose or ears as far as he can see but huge eyes as black as space and an elongated mouth almost as long as the snout that houses rows of razor-sharp teeth.

"Charlie Davenport," it squeals, what looks to be a child's backpack clasped in its left claw.

Charlie pushes back against the wall again. "Help!"

The creature offers another squeal, and Charlie helplessly watches as it begins sprinkling the contents of the pack on the ground: A small shoe, a hairbrush, a Rubik's Cube, candy bar wrappers, a Polaroid camera, and a host of other paraphernalia, most of which look like they once belonged to a kid like you, Charlie.

A large book is the last thing to drop, helped by the creature turning the pack inside out as it offers a series of excited squeals. It crouches, clumsily flicking the pages over. "Charlie Davenport."

"Let me go, please. I'll tell no one. Promise!" So many children, perhaps a dozen photographs to each page—and the book so thick. "Please!" The tears begin, but he can see clearly enough as the creature flattens the sheet and starts tapping one of its blades in the centre of the only golden frame. A light monochrome version of himself smiles proudly from within, and beneath, in thick black ink, his name is printed in a strange font full of flicks and curls.

"Smile," the creature squeals, bringing the Polaroid to its face.

The camera bathes Charlie in white light, capturing a boy at the height of fear, a kid who knows there'll be no intervention from the gods, no celebration, no fish for tea, no kiss from Amy Winters, no walking Basil tonight.

As Mole Man wafts the print in the air, squealing with anticipation, Charlie glances at the card sitting atop the branches and grass, his mind full of death and one crazy thought that he can't shake.

At least I was a gold.

THROUGH HER EYES

Standing in the doorway, squinting into daylight that she rarely sees these days, my daughter Fiona watches me cleaning the car. She's probably judging, too—a bin bag full of countless coffee cups and takeaway cartons—hardly a snapshot of a life to be proud of.

Feeling the irony after insisting yesterday we take the drive together; I offer a smile. "Ready, darling?"

Over recent days she's become more sullen than usual. Today, she looks especially withdrawn and exhausted, pallid skin emphasizing sunken eyes. Sometimes I stand by her bedroom door, listening to her tossing and turning, crying, moaning, and occasionally muttering to herself. It breaks my heart. Her mother's death hit her for six, and I feel like a helpless bystander, witnessing an echo of who she once was. She saunters over to the car and slinks into the seat without a word.

Isn't time supposed to heal, not let things bleed out?

Jenny's voice plays in my head. *Look through her eyes, not yours.* Judging. Always fucking judging.

Emptying the box of rubbish into the already full recycle bin only compounds self-disgust. It was all couscous and fresh veg when Jenny was around. I tried for a while, I really did, but just like with my marriage, it wasn't long before I started with the short-cuts.

Always looking for the easy route was another of Jenny's favourites.

We were seeing a counsellor when Jenny got the diagnosis. Umpteen sessions in, but we seemed to be sinking further into each other's misery. If truth be told, I think news of the illness only made her resent me more, that she would be spending her last few weeks with someone she no longer respected.

I fall back into the driver's seat, feeling like giving up before even starting.

"Where are we going anyway?" Fiona finally says, no eye contact, staring straight ahead, wearing her face like a declaration of war.

"You might want to shut your door first."

She refuses to move, lips pursed, not even a blink.

"I'll do it then!" I thrust myself from the car, making a big deal of marching to her side. It happens even quicker these days: the accelerated heart rate, the bass playing in my ears, the fizzing in my veins. By the time I get there, I'm ready to slam that door so fucking hard she'll have to give me something. Instead, I count to three and let the door go, declining her invitation.

Damned if I'll fail before I begin. "I don't know, love," I say softly, getting back into the driver's side. "Away from all the distractions, just you and me."

She crosses her arms and snaps her head to the left. "Sounds like a riot."

"Seatbelt, darling."

Nothing.

She recoils as I reach over, fastening her in, her face twisting into a scowl as cold as her aura. Holding my tongue, I start the engine and slowly bring the car out of the weed-infested driveway, noting how morose the house looks these days, also a shadow of its former self.

"How's school?"

She offers a deep sigh. "Is this what we're going to talk about?"

"I'm just interested. How's Tara?"

"Who's Tara?"

"Your friend."

"Clara?" You mean Clara?" She offers a muted laugh and angles even further away. "Clara's dead to me."

"What has got into you of late?" I say, restrained as possible.

All that's missing is a cigarette and a tumbler of whisky. I try my best, biting my lip through her reticence, but the words bounce relentlessly and violently in my head. "I said what the hell has got into you!"

"There you are, Daddy! I wondered where you'd gone."

Streets are packed full of families enjoying the first day of the school holidays, or at least pretending to. Regardless, smiles and projected contentment take us further towards an inevitable crescendo.

"I'm doing my best, Fi."

It's weak, I know, and it gets the silence it deserves.

As we leave the city behind, the smell of wildflowers and manure begins displacing some of the heaviness, and it's tempting to hope the air will just blow it all away. The mere thought only lends weight to Jenny's case—still winning from six feet under. Weeks have passed since Cancer finally finished the job, and so far, Fi and I have only gone through the motions. She won't talk, detests my touch, and even getting her to look at me is a battle. The conversation is more than a little overdue.

"We need to talk about things."

Sensing what is coming, she re-folds her arms and directs her gaze to the line of trees.

"She would have wanted us to get on, Fi; talk things through." I feel my fingers tightening around the wheel as she mumbles something under her breath. "Fi, I said—"

"You haven't got a clue what she wanted!"

The bass intensifies, fingers coiled so tightly they begin to ache.

Through her eyes.

"I understand, Fi. I know how close you both were."

"You were never here."

Always looking for an easy route.

"Now, that's not true, Fi. I was—"

"Sleeping with the tart from work," she says, finally snapping her head towards me.

Shock ties my brain in knots as I open my mouth to speak, only managing a garbled croak. I can still feel her eyes on me. "What's wrong, Daddy? She would have wanted us to talk things through."

Bland colours merge into one as I try and focus on the thin strip of grey ahead. I knew it was never going to be easy, but this!

"Mummy was hurting, Daddy. Hurting so bad. How could you do such a thing?"

Easy route.

I told Jenny. I couldn't live with myself. But I can't believe she would tell Fi—that she would leave us with this. "Your mother and I talked about it. I made a big mistake, Fi. A colossal one. I ended it as soon as Mum got sick. I—"

"That's what you told, Mum, but you didn't end it, did you? And Mommy knew."

I was so tired, beside myself with grief and worry, *and she* listened. I tried to end it, but I got so lonely, so w*eak*. She made me feel like I was more than just a carer and a father, as though I was a whole person with needs and wants of my own.

"I swear, Fi, it—"

"Mommy said you'd try and squirm from the truth. What kind of man cheats on their dying wife, Daddy?"

Guilt and discomposure twist my insides as I search for words. How did Jenny know that I saw her again? Did she have people watching me? We were careful. So careful.

"She was surprised you told her in the first place, but I guess from her death bed, there wasn't a lot she could do."

"Fi, I—"

"Don't you think that's weak, Daddy?"

"Stop it, Fi."

"Stop what? We're just talking things through, aren't we, Daddy? That's what you wanted, isn't it, Daddy?"

Blood pounds in my head, and I can taste blood at the back of my mouth. The heavy canopy above locks in the dimness, and I see no light ahead.

"Come on, Daddy! Let's chew the fat, shoot the shit, spill the beans."

The sequence throws me, but she's always been an avid reader like her mum, picking up slang, throwing down lines. Jenny could disarm me anytime she wanted with a quote from one of the many self-help books that littered the house.

"Okay, Fi, okay." I take in the heavy cologne of the surrounding woods, forcing myself into relative composure. The crows caw impatiently as if anxiously awaiting the show. "Your mother and I have been struggling for a while. We were—"

"Young when you were married. Mother said you'd try that bull-shit."

My teeth dig further into my lip, and my knuckles turn stark white against the black plastic. It sounds as if the crows are mocking me now.

"Sorry, Daddy, carry on. But I think you can do better."

I think you can do better. One of Jenny's favourites that drove me through the fucking roof.

Inhale. Exhale. Inhale. Exhale. "Sometimes, people change, and expectations can—"

The crackle of laughter surprises me. She puts one hand to her mouth and frantically waves the other towards me as if I'm a little more than hilarious. My instinct is to scream at her to stop, but I've no control here. She has it all.

Goddamn fucking crows!

Finally, she wipes a tear from her right eye and recomposes. "You're a hoot, Daddy. It's just like Mommy said it would be."

I don't even know where we are anymore. *Ain't that the truth.* "What do you mean by that? Like Mommy said it would be."

"Oh, she's been coming to see me. Said she couldn't stand being apart, so she came back."

My mind races with responses, but I resist.

Through her eyes.

"Sweetheart, I know you want that more than anything in the world, but your mum is gone. Deep down, you know she can't come back. The dead can't come back." I can't very well leave it like that. "But I promise you'll see her again one day."

"Your promises mean as much to me as they did to her."

Inhale. Three. Two. One. Exhale. "Fi, I'm not perfect. I'm flawed. But your mum wasn't the—"

"Don't you dare," she says through gritted teeth.

We're no further on, possibly in a worse place than before, and now I have the conjuring of her mother to contend with. Fuuuuuuuuck!

The road is getting windier and hillier, and the canopy above is thicker than ever, an abundance of dancing crows blocking out even further light.

Don't try and fix it. Just listen. I hated that she was right all the time. "How long has she been coming back for?" I relax my grip on the wheel.

Fi lets out a deep sigh, but her body loosens. "Only recently. I prayed every night, but last week, she stepped out of the shadows for the first time."

This could be it, the connection. "What did she look like? I mean, was she—"

"Like an angel."

"What did she say?"

"She said a lot."

"Like what?"

"That you always resented having a child."

My hope fades. "No. That's simply not true. Absolutely—"

"You wanted an abortion."

My mind struggles to keep up. I'm out of depth and sinking fast. "I was just young, but I swear I never regret having you. I love you!"

"I swear, I swear. Do you swear you never had a drinking problem, too, Daddy?"

This fucking goddamn road is endless!

"And that you never stayed at work just to avoid us? Do you swear that you never refused to take the paid leave your boss offered? That you never cursed the day you ever met her, Daddy?"

"Enough, Fi!"

"That you wished she would just get on and die!"

The crows are deafening now, hopping from one foot to the next, an excitable audience watching the carnage unfold. I open my mouth to defend myself, but I have nothing.

"Don't you want to talk anymore, Daddy?"

This drive was supposed to fix things, heal wounds and bring us closer together, but I feel even further apart. It doesn't make sense. Differences aside, I can't imagine Jenny ever putting her daughter through this much pain, feeding her with this bile. It just wasn't part—

"Daddy?"

"When did she tell you all this, Fi?"

"I told you; she's been coming to see me. Came last night, too."

Feeling a sudden chill, I wind the window up, but it doesn't help. My skin crawls and tightens; I'm trembling. Can't think straight, can't focus, the crows only slightly dampened cries continuing from gnarly branches. I don't know how to deal with any of this.

"She asked me if I wanted to stay with her."

I'm so fucking cold, yet I feel beads of sweat rolling down my cheeks as violence erupts within. I want to roar, drown everything out. My hairs bristle, and blood pulses relentlessly across my forehead. "Your mother's dead, Fi."

"To you, maybe."

How the fuck am I supposed to deal with this? "Fi, we watched her wither away to nothing. She's in a box underground, and there's no coming back."

She shakes her head. "I've seen her, felt her breath against me."

I'm losing it, sinking into a quagmire of confused anger, and there's nothing I can do. "Fi, she's as dead as dead can be. Taking a dirt nap. A bag of bones and an ounce of fucking gristle." My fist slams into the centre of the steering wheel, sending the horn blaring and birds flapping wildly from their branches into the road. "Nothing but fucking worm food!"

Fi's sullen and pale face remains unchanged, much like her mother's used to after one of my childish outbursts. She clears her throat. "I said yes, Daddy. I'm going to stay with Mummy."

It's unfair—that I need to deal with this kind of fallout. "Stop this nonsense, Fi!" I snap my foot down hard on the accelerator to take us up the rise of a hill.

"She kissed me, Daddy."

"Stop it, Fi!"

"Breathed me in. Left just enough for today."

"Please stop talking like this. Just stop it, Fi!"

"Insisted I came for the drive to say goodbye."

I turn to her, noticing her skin even paler than before against the black fabric. "For fuck's sake. Fi!"

"But I have to go now; Mommy said the veil is closing."

"Fi, will you please just shut the—"

"Daddy!"

As I instinctively bring the wheel hard left, my mind takes a delayed snapshot of the bottom of the hill: half-a-dozen crows basking in the spotlight of sun, a grotesque and withered body at their centre. But the face—

To the sound of twisting metal, the world becomes a furious kaleidoscope of greens and browns. I'm weightless, surrounded by floating glass. Grimacing for pain, I close my eyes, the soundtrack of violence bleeding into my ears.

It feels like it will never end. Until it does.

My head roars. My insides are on fire. Silence prevails, bar the sound of spinning tyres. I unscrew my eyes to see a thick branch protruding from the centre of my chest like a deformed extra limb. Something's leaking inside. "Fi!"

Nothing.

"Fi." Pain fires up my arm as I give her a gentle shove. "Fi!"

Her head lollops to the side. A string of saliva extends towards the floor.

"Fi, please."

The wheels stop spinning. Even the crows are quiet now. And strangely, my pain is beginning to subside. I reach towards her colourless body and feel for a pulse. Not a mark on her, but she's—gone.

Breathed me in. Left just enough for today.

And in the rear-view mirror, I see her amongst the crows, ethereally hovering over the carcass. She reaches towards the body, and a frail spindly arm lifts from the ground.

Jenny's face. But that isn't her.

"Fi, no!"

As my little girl helps the *thing* to its feet, it coils its spindly fingers around one of her shoulders and brings her in close. It looks towards the car as if to gloat, covered in a cloak of spiralling dark mist. It isn't her; anyone could see it, perhaps aside from a grieving daughter.

Through her eyes.

Only a rasp emerges as I scream after Fi. I feel nothing now, numb, and I know I'm on borrowed time as I watch the *thing* that stepped out from the shadows leading my daughter away. I can see the trees through Fi's midriff, only slightly distorted by the black wisps of cloud surrounding her, courtesy of the darkness to her right. Tugging at the spindly arm protruding from the blackness, Fi turns and offers a solemn wave. It turns, too, this vile incarnation that feeds on misery, grief, and death.

All that poison it fed her, all that hate. What evil would do such a thing?

And what a swan song.

It offers a final smile before they both disappear behind the veil of black fog.

Hugh's Friend

When I speak to my friends, we often joke and reminisce about the past. One such time, we chatted about the imaginary friends we used to have as kids and how we would play or discuss things with them, even occasionally arguing with them. Perhaps it was just an intuitive way of preparing ourselves for growing up.

Hugh was my imaginary so-called friend.

The general rule of thumb was that they would come out on request—when you wanted to play or just not be alone. Hugh was an exception to this rule. A bit of a prick, if I'm being honest.

Example:

We were sitting at the dinner table one day, and as my mum was reaching for the veggies, he slipped under the table. Almost immediately, he came back up, holding his nose and gagging before telling me that mum "wasn't wearing any knickers." I intentionally dropped my fork to prove he was telling tales. That vision still haunts me today.

Some things he told me were truths, and others were just outright lies designed to ruin self-confidence and push anxiety levels through the roof. Hugh found such taunting to be hilarious. For example, on my eighth birthday, he told me I was adopted, and the papers were in the third drawer of my mum's dresser. All I found was a bunch of knickers and bras and what looked to be a torch that vibrated. Hugh went on to tell me that my mum used to shove said 'torch' so far up her "doodaa" you could see her tonsils. I didn't believe a word he said after all that business.

Further claims, such as my mum was sleeping with the postman and that my dad was a serial killer, fell on deaf ears. He even said he could prove it, but I'd had enough by then. For weeks, I tried to unimagine him from my mind, but it became obvious the stubborn little 'prick' wasn't ready to leave.

The first day at school, already a hard enough time for an eight-year-old to get their heads around, was something I will never forget. The teacher placed me next to a kid called Robert. He seemed nice enough, but Hugh seemed almost jealous that I'd even said "hello" to him.

In my ear all day, "You're a homo, you're a homo," and slightly more inventive, "Jack and Bobby sitting in a tree, Jack blows Bobby, one-two-three."

That carried on all day, "You're a homo, you're a homo," until I lost the plot and screamed at the top of my lungs in front of the entire classroom, "I'm not a fucking homo!"

Some kids laughed, and some went white. The teacher did neither but did escort me from the class.

Mum picked me up early. She said she was "very disappointed." In contrast, Hugh was unbelievably pleased with himself.

Later that day, when Mum popped out for a chat with the neighbour, Hugh asked me to follow him because he wanted to show me something.

"Where are we going?" I called out to him in pursuit as he sprinted down the hallway towards the house's back end.

"You'll see soon enough," he replied, reaching the cellar door.

My dad always said the cellar was a work in progress and too dangerous for us to enter. I always wondered why it didn't apply to him, though.

"Hugh, I am not allowed in there; even Mum isn't!"

"Do you ever think to yourself, why not?" he asked, pointing to a jar on top of the cupboard. I was admittedly quite surprised when the key fell out. Anyway, I grabbed it and unlocked the door. The air conditioner was already on; I still recall the cool blast. There's a lot I remember about that day.

When I flicked the light switch on, nothing happened.

"Oh yes, in the cupboard next to the door," Hugh said.

After going back and grabbing a normal-looking torch from the drawer, I felt along the walls and followed the beam, noting the vast array of jars and bottles of wine across various tables.

"What are we doing here, Hugh?" I asked impatiently.

"Keep going, nearly there," he replied.

I kept edging along the wall until I finally came to the end of the room. "What?" I asked, flashing the torch but seeing nothing noteworthy.

"Push that last panel, Jack," he said.

I did, and it moved inwards, not just a little bit. I soon realised it was a makeshift door.

"How do you know all this, Hugh?"

"Go inside, Jack."

As I stepped across the threshold, sweeping the torch around, I shrieked and dropped it. In a mix of fear and panic, I scrambled on the floor, finally feeling the handle and pointing it forward again. The little boy in the corner of the room covered his eyes until I moved the torch out of his direct line of sight. As he cowered, I noticed the chain attached to the bolt on the floor and a plate and glass on the adjacent mattress.

"This is Peter," Hugh replied very casually.

"Why are you in our house, Peter?" I asked very naively.

Peter didn't say anything. He just sat shaking.

"You need to ask your dad," Hugh replied.

As I turned around to shine the torch towards Hugh, I saw the etchings on the wooden interior of the room.

Hugh was here.

The end

She's Dead

She's dead. Behind the eyes, I mean.

She moves the items over the barcode scanner with undeniable poetry, but it isn't rocket science. For a moment, I consider the idea of a checkout monkey. A little giggle sneaks out, but alas, nothing from—what is her name? Bethany. That's the name on the badge anyway. What a funny name that would be for a chimp. And then I think, what wouldn't be? Monica? Marge?

The explosion sends me to the floor, a thunderclap of shattered glass. I feel some of it pierce the right side of my body, but no pain registers. There's a ringing in my ears. Blood begins to seep through my crisp white shirt, and I wonder how I'll ever get it out.

I see someone slowly get up—a young man, perhaps in his twenties. He dusts himself off with his good hand. His other arm is on the floor next to a green basket. He glances around, and I follow his gaze across the debris. We catch sight of each other. I have never seen him before, yet I feel close to him.

My body starts to sting as the shock wears off. Slowly, I push myself up to see the conveyor belt covered in broken glass. I'll need to put that lettuce back.

I turn to face Bethany. Her face is a mess, cut to shreds by shards of glass that remain embedded in her skin; they sparkle in the evening sun like diamonds.

I start to move towards her, and she looks directly at me for the first time. Something isn't right. Shock can affect people in different ways, but her eyes are as dead as they were before. No sign of trauma. She turns back to the conveyor belt, picks up the juice, puts it through, and then roughly grabs the lettuce and asks if I want to change it for another.

The ringing in my ear starts to subside, and I can hear the sounds of people screaming and crying for help.

Bethany has just asked if I want to change my lettuce.

I scream at her then, "What's wrong with you?"

"It has a caterpillar on it," she replies sheepishly.

"Are you insane, woman?" I scream at her again.

For the first time, I see some fear in her eyes. It gives me some satisfaction.

Someone is pulling at my shirt, "Hey, buddy, are you okay?"

I turn around to see the guy from earlier, but any feeling of closeness has gone. He is unscathed, unmarked, and has both arms intact.

The manager approaches the next checkout with a broom and starts sweeping the broken jar from the floor.

It's happened again.

I need help. I've been back for three months, but it isn't getting any better. I'm beginning to wonder if it ever will.

I look towards the street outside and can see the enemy all around. The reflection in the window projects a much younger version of myself—gun in hand, full uniform—ready for action.

The end

Devil's Ink

It's been nearly four weeks since I last put pen to paper. Each day that passes, the disconnect seems to grow, and I'm worried I might not find a way back. Elly says it's because I'm locking myself away from life. She challenges me. "How can the promising new find, Tristan Kowalski, conjure new worlds if he doesn't even acknowledge his own?" The Last time Elly visited; I told her not to come back—that I needed space. She may be happy enough swimming in mediocrity with only minor flashes of anything credible, but I'm not. Sacrifices must be made.

The view is usually enough to inspire: rolling hills, decrepit farm buildings, skies that carry a bounty of orange and gold endlessly stretching into the distance. Yet here I am, pen in hand and a headful of second-rate ideas to embarrass me. Of late, I don't feel worthy of the pen, as though its beauty undermines me; solid gold, ornately decorated with all sorts of other-worldly scenes, and the words "For Tristan" etched down one side. We've done great work together, but now I find myself clasping it tightly like a weapon rather than a tool, full of rage and impatience.

I have nothing. Nothing!

Slamming my fist into the desk, I let out a scream—a wild maniacal cry of hopeless desperation that echoes through the house. Even the crows outside take flight, cawing their noisy disapproval.

And it happens—just like that—a moment of unequivocal clarity.

It's as though the crows have lifted the veil of bile and fogginess that has been shrouding my brain in recent weeks. The idea is forming. I can feel the adrenaline kicking in—heart rate increasing, goosebumps randomly prickling across my skin, and the pen shaking in my grasp.

As if on cue, a haunting wind whistles across the front of the house. The rotting sash windows gently rattle in their frames, and through the glass, I watch the dark clouds roll in impossibly quickly, swallowing sunlight and the innocence of day. It's a much more sinister scene, and it sends a shudder down my spine. I've felt this before, a sudden shift of energy. But not like this; never this powerful.

It's as though something is here with me.

Nestled between the bandages, painkillers, anticoagulants, and medical tape is the confronting but exhilarating sight of the fresh steel blade. Hand still shaking, I purse my fingers around it and delicately roll up my left sleeve. Partially healed wounds from my last success still appear sore, and the entire arm is still tender to touch, nerve endings screaming in protest as I tentatively search for unblemished areas. I try the other arm, but hard scar tissue weaves its way from the wrist to bicep—needlework isn't a strong point of mine. Unbuckling my belt, I slide it from around my waist and undo the button of my pants. They fall to the ground, revealing more of my handy work. Finally, I find some untouched flesh on the underside of my thigh and ready myself, doubling up the belt and placing it between my teeth.

"Why do you insist on using red ink?" my publisher once asked.

I was taken to the edge with the last story—couldn't tell you how much blood I poured into that one, but it was worth it. I know how far I can go and which veins to avoid.

The familiar bitter earthiness of the belt gathers at the back of my throat as I try to steady my hand. Three—two—one. I run the blade across my thigh and wince at the slightly delayed pain, watching as the crimson begins to trickle down my pale skin. Pushing it further in, I twist the blade, biting down hard as pulses of torment vibrate down my leg.

Christ above!

Deep breaths, Tristan; look beyond the pain and think of what you are achieving.

I dip the pen into the beautiful redness and quickly begin to scribe the first few words across the paper. Relief is immediate as the taunting blankness gives way to lines of prose that make me want to laugh and cry. I'm in the zone, on a roll, unstoppable.

I'm not insane. This is no ordinary pen, you see. It was a gift left for me on my bedside table—perhaps by the same entity here with me now. I can't recall much about her appearance other than the yellow eyes and black cloak, but her words resonated with me. It must be nearly ten years since she visited me in my sleep, telling me how much she admired my work. Her only critique was that my stories could often feel detached, full of redundant words and superficial ramblings rather than accurate depictions of a character's actions or emotional state.

"You are doing yourself an injustice," she had said.

She told me the pen was magic, that it would change my life forever. There were rules, though. It must be human blood, freshly drawn to be effective, and I could only moderate the pain with household painkillers. Anything beyond this would tarnish the emotional raw-ness and overall effectiveness. The blood would provide a life source for the pen that would take it beyond simple calligraphy, enchanting it with an intuition that would know what to write even before I could conjure the words. All I needed was the idea, and the pen would do the rest, allowing my characters to bleed onto the paper.

I've already filled four pages, but I want to make sure I can set a maintainable pace. I wrap some tape around my wound and relax back into the chair, watching as the clouds begin to roll back. A morsel of light finds its way through the grimy window as I break off some bread and wash four painkillers down with a glass of Chianti. It almost feels as though the presence has left now that I have stopped writing.

I don't need to re-read my work. It is perfection. And when I'm finished with this one, everyone will know who Tristan Kowalski is.

My leg pulsates with a satisfying dull throb, but for me, pain means productivity. It means I am working and creating, that I am happy. I knock back the wine and pour another glass.

"Here's to the one they will remember forever," I toast.

*

Startled, I wake up in the chair, throat dry, my neck stiff. Grabbing my wooden cane, I push myself to my feet and hobble carefully to the bathroom.

My face is free of cuts but tired looking: pale skin with a tinge of yellow, dark circles, and sunken eyes. I carefully lift the gauze to inspect the wound—it shouldn't be too painful to reopen. After splashing my face with cold water, I return to my desk and slowly ease into the chair.

Almost immediately, morning light fades.

As I work the blade back into my skin, teeth clenched, the brighter blood begins to spill over the darkened surface. I can't afford to waste a drop, so I quickly gather the pen and dip it in.

And I'm off.

I have often asked myself if it is cheating, but all the magic pen does is bring out what is already inside of me. I come up with the idea, and the pen only helps in the transition from mind to paper. Besides, something this arduous and painful surely could not be considered cheating. I was gifted this by someone—or something—who believed in me. What am I to do?

Paragraph after paragraph, page after page, I write as though trying to rid my mind of bile. I've no idea what time it is, clouds remaining consistently grey, the clock in pieces at my feet. How many painkillers have I have taken? I've no clue; all I know is the emotional charge jumping from the page transcends any of the pain. Six wounds gape open on my right leg, but there is a detachment as though I am on a different plain.

So much for pacing myself!

I'm halfway through the story, but I'm growing weary. I have started to see things—shadows lurking in the dingy corners of the room—and in the middle of the field, the scarecrow appears to be slowly rotating.

*

I wake up to see a pool of semi-congealed blood surrounding the chair. Shit, how much blood have I wasted? Why the fuck didn't I wrap my wounds? I have to be on top of this; otherwise, I won't make it. Pain is sharp but manageable. Six painkillers should do it; any more would make my attempts at writing futile. I can only rely on the pen so much.

My body is sluggish—heavy and unresponsive, but if I work all day, perhaps I can finish this dark tale. Groans emerge from my stomach, but any hunger pangs are overridden by the tremendous pain that rips down my leg as I raise myself from the chair. Carefully, I strip off my blood-soaked clothes, grimacing with each move. I'm numb to the devastation I've inflicted on my body, but scar tissue across my skin means prostitutes demand a premium. Don't judge me; my love is for my work, and sacrifices must be made.

I grab the blade and urgently survey the uneven landscape of my skin until I find an untouched clearing. With the belt between my teeth once more, I rip through the right side of my abdomen and release a garbled muffled scream. Fuuuucckkkk! The blood comes out fast; I think I've gone too deep. No time to waste, I grab the pen and go to work, paying no heed to the rattles of the windows or the darkness that wraps itself around the house.

A complexity of emotions flows onto the paper. Nothing is lost in translation as the pen dances across the pages, bringing heartache and despair to these real people I have created. I feel it all, and I know the reader will, too. Not one mistake, no edits required—a flawless account of darkness.

Wait. What was that? Something in the room. More shadows.

The words on the page begin to drift in and out of focus. I feel light-headed.

No—not now.

Everywhere I look, I see my blood, fresh, congealed, in-between. So much of it. Has my urgency made me careless? I must finish it today, though! Then I can heal, rest, bask in the inevitable glory.

I carry on—nobody said it would be easy. The scratching on the paper is no longer satisfying. Each stroke feels as though I am drawing the sharp nib across my nerve endings. My body screams at me to stop, but the composition continues.

Tears roll down my cheek as I continue to scrawl—a combination of pain and the beauty of the prose that spills. I'm so close now. My mind is starting to play tricks on me; the paper, replaced with human skin, and the scarecrow outside appears to be getting closer each time.

Is it smiling?

There's a cacophony of crows, but I can't see any through the window.

I sink the pen into my chest and grimace at the raw pain that lights me up. My arm feels weak now, and it hurts to hold the pen, but the words carry on. Eyes closing, body throbbing, the final chapter is shaping up nicely. I'm drifting in and out of consciousness, but the ending is coming together in heart-rending scenes of exquisite distress. A couple more pages and I should be—

*

The crows wake me.

I must have passed out again. They scream in my head like some twisted alarm I can't turn off. *Come on!*

My body wants to give up, switch off, but the partnership continues—the pen narrating my inner darkness. These characters are self-destructing, their hate eating them from the inside. And it's magical.

So close—I'm on the last page—this is where it ends.

Is that in my head? The low hum of an engine above the caws. It's getting louder.

Must focus. But fuck, I feel as though I'm losing it.

Words still flow, but each one is becoming more laborious. I am struggling to keep pace. The sheet of paper suddenly seems impossibly far away. Black spots dance in front of my eyes in rhythm to the pulsating pain. Shadows float across my vision, and that mysterious presence feels ever stronger. And the crows—so impossibly loud.

A thundering knock on the door startles me. My imagination? No. As if in agreement, the crows instantly cease their cries and the shadows leave.

"Tristan," the voice is slow and distorted, but I still recognize it as Elly's.

No. Go away.

Why did the jealous bitch have to come now?

Another knock. "Tristan, I know you're in there."

Please leave.

I am so weak. I'm not sure how long I can keep going.

The sound of crunching gravel brings some relief—she's leaving. I try to regroup for the final push. But she's at the window, her face drawn back in concern and disgust.

"Tristan!" she screams, running down the side of the house

The door. Fuck—I don't think it's locked.

Within seconds, it swings open. I scowl at her unwelcome presence. Cavernous lines eat into her bloodless face as she cries, "What have you done?"

"It's fine. I'm nearly finished," I say impatiently.

"You need a hospital. You're a mess." She wraps an arm around my shoulder as if to escort me away but only manages to partially turn the chair.

"Leave me alone!"

"Look at the blood!" she asserts. "You're going to die."

"Fuck off!" My lips curl back around my teeth.

"I'm calling an ambulance," she says.

My tolerance is exhausted.

As she momentarily releases her grip to reach into her handbag, I swing the pen with as much force as I can muster into her neck. Instinctively, she reaches towards her throat with little facial reaction, but as the shock and realization kick in, she drops to her knees, eyes wide and full of terror. Whimpering follows—no rage, no screams—just a series of pathetic moans. Muted disbelief projects from her eyes, and I can only imagine the internal rush of thoughts in her head that throw her mortality into question.

She wraps her fingers around the pen and rips it out, creating a fountain of blood that sprays to the floor below. I watch her body topple over into the shallow pool of crimson, wincing at the thud of her head on the floor. A lengthy and horrific gurgle leaves her lips as she squirms in our combined cocktail of blood.

Until a heavy silence blankets the room.

Without hesitation, I reach for the pen, grimacing at the waves of pain that rush over me. I've lost too much blood. Elly was right; I'm going to die.

The words start to flow once again as the crows pick up their raucous tune. There's a stench in the room, too—perhaps the smell of my imminent death. But I am down to the last paragraph; nothing can stop me now. The shadows that fill my vision are becoming more aggressive, more restless, as though excited about the imminent climax of the tale.

Forcing my eyes to remain open as my entire body vibrates with a raw sensitivity, I write the first few words of the ending. More tears break through as the story nears its harrowing conclusion.

The smell is getting worse—putrid, like nothing I've experienced before. Sinister darkness fills the room that I know can't be attributed to the clouds alone. Urgently, I dip the pen back into Elly's neck and begin the final sentence.

Shadows peel away from the walls, surrounding me in a series of black clouds that aggressively splinter into smaller ones and regroup.

An oppressive heaviness weighs down on me. Is this what dying feels like?

I push on with the final few words. It will be finished.

And out of the black mist steps the familiar figure—hooded black cloak draping across her human form—yellow eyes on me, but only darkness surrounding them. "Finish," her low guttural voice prompts.

My life is dwindling away. I feel it. But as I write the last few words, I cannot help but smile. I've done it—my masterpiece.

"The end," I announce.

"It's been a long time, Tristan," the entity says.

"It's perfect," is all I can conjure. "Perfect."

"Do you know who I am?"

"The pen—you gave me the magic pen?"

"I did," she says. "But it isn't magic."

"What? What are you talking about?"

"How else could I induce such passion and intensity without raising the stakes?" she replies.

"It's not—not magic?"

"It's just a pen. You wrote this, felt this, bled this. No words wasted, no redundant branches of prose. I've been here with you, watching your new-found mastery of words. You're ready now."

"But—why did you lie? And ready for what?"

"I am the devil—and I lie. I just had to be sure you were the one."

The crows are back, but this time I can see them. They're in my room, fluttering wildly above our heads.

"You see, I need a writer. Someone to document my work, to portray the fear and torment I create. God has the Bible, but I have nothing. You'll be my writer, and together, we we'll make history."

Piercing caws emerge from the crows as they launch into aggressive swoops—like vultures impatiently waiting for their dying prey. My heart rate slows, my life ebbing away.

At least they'll remember me for this piece.

She looks almost sympathetic as she clicks her fingers, creating a large orange flame that dances in the palm of her hands.

Not my manuscript. "No, pleeeaassseeee—"

And as the crows drag my soul away from the shell of the body on the floor, I watch the pages burn.

Eric's Tune

The last members of the group shuffle out, leaving just Jen and me in the starkness of the cell. I take a moment to breathe in the deceiving vastness of the damp air, considering the hell it must have been to be held in this prison for real. "Go on, Jen," I say, waving her out. "Out the cell and close the door." My skin tingles, some excitement perhaps, but I can't deny the prickle of fear as my head falls against the cold concrete.

"I honestly don't think this a good idea, Jake."

"Come on; it's too good not to. Don't be a killjoy."

"Damn it, Jake; I already feel bad for making her come. She and Max aren't exactly hitting it off."

"Never a good idea to set up your friends, Jen, especially when they're as dorky as... "

"It's Max, and he's just shy."

"Not with you. Anyway, think of it as an icebreaker, something they can talk about over dinner. Go on, quick."

She sighs, a hand on her hip, giving me the crinkled forehead and wide eyes that suggest I may live to regret this. Bec should know better; a late-night tour of an old prison with yours truly for company. It's asking for trouble.

"We'll be laughing about it over a few drinks soon. Go on, will you? Make sure you close the cell door all the way." The chill of the concrete is already spreading. I readjust, but it doesn't help; I guess it's the price you pay for comedy.

"You're a fucking child," she mutters on the way out.

"I know."

As the dim light from the corridor begins to fade, I arch my neck towards the slither of moonlight filtering through the tiny, barred window. I have an immediate craving for warm food. As my stomach gives out a loud rumble, my eyes begin to adjust, giving the impression the walls are closing in. The clang of the door sends a shiver down my spine.

I can't deny the uneasiness that washes over me as Jen's footsteps fade into the distance until I'm left with only the moans of my stomach for company. Being in a cell alone in almost complete darkness, laying across a concrete bed used likely by all sorts of miscreants, certainly makes for a more immersive experience, but I'm beginning to feel a little too close to it all.

As I lay my head back again, a titter of laughter echoes down the corridor bringing some relief. Eyes wide open, I listen to the under-appreciated chatter of law-abiding humans.

"And this, ladies and gents," the tour guide's now distant voice announces, "is where the vilest of them all were kept. Nasty pieces of work that would make you question humanity: murderers, rapists, and that's just touching the surface. Some of these criminals did things that would likely have them thrown out of Hell itself."

"Like what?" I hear someone holler.

"These cells housed the likes of Ted Kafferty, Norman Jones, William Eisenberg, and Leonard Thomas, to name a few. Look them up in your own time, but there are things even I'm not prepared to broach, a certain type of dark that we should never glorify."

More nervous chatter breaks out among the group. "Good pitch," someone comments to a ripple of forced laughter.

"It feels colder here," someone else comments.

"People have said that before," the guide says. "Some have even claimed to feel a presence."

"Were they allowed out? For exercise, I mean?"

"Thirty minutes a day, always alone. Shackled, of course, which meant movement was limited."

"Bring back those days. Like bloody hotels, prisons are, now."

"Didn't stop Leonard Thomas from escaping, though; somehow managing to break free and scale the walls. He always insisted he was innocent and that they'd got the wrong man."

"So, he could still be out there somewhere?" someone asks.

"He'd likely be dead now. This way, please; I don't like to linger in this wing."

"What did he do?" A man's voice this time. I think it's the guy with red cheeks and a belly like a cannonball.

I hear the lady give a loud sniff. "What didn't he do should be the question."

The piercing scream that fills the building is deafening, but the raucous laughter that follows lets me know there's another prankster in the group.

"You fucking idiot, John!"

"It wasn't me, love. It must have been that Ted bloke! He's come back for seconds."

"With haste, please," the tour guide firmly beckons. "I have another group at eight."

Body rigid, I ready myself. No real plan, just a moaning wail might do it, or I could even flip upright and growl. Either way, it will be a hoot. I listen for the door, face screwed up in excited anticipation, but there's only mumbling from the corridor and footsteps chasing the lady with the clipboard.

As I shift position on the concrete, a breeze sneaks through the opening above, dropping its cold blanket, causing my skin to crawl. Come on, Jen! Only the sound of my breathing now for company; part of me already wants to call it a day, to get up and speed walk out of the room.

So damned cold in here

Above my head, I note a shallow indent in the wall. I trace my fingers across it. An L, is it? And is this a T next to it? Yes! LT.

Wait! What did—ah, shit—what was her name again? Viola? Violet? She said one of the guys on the wing was called Leonard, but what was the second name?

I begin to imagine what he might have used to mark the wall. Was he lying down in this exact spot? What was going through his head at the time? A resignation to his fate? A permanent marking to designate the tiny room as his home for life?

You were a naughty boy, Leonard. "What did you do?"

The sudden warmth against my neck makes me jolt upright, heart-pounding. "Jesus fuckity fuck!"

As I snap my head around, the walls seem to close in a little more. Not a drop of saliva in my mouth, I push myself from the concrete bed, shivering as another bluster embraces me. "See you around, Len." Peering through the small-barred slot of the metal door, just in case

Jen is still working on Bec, I see only darkness; no sign of the group at all, not even a straggler.

The fuck?

I push the door, but it doesn't budge. "Oh, yes, well played, Jen!" I try again, but it's going nowhere. "Okay, Jen, you win."

My skin crawls, an icy blanket wrapping around me.

"Very good. Joke's on me."

I glance over my shoulder, purely paranoia, the room feeling smaller still. They're never going to let me live this down. "You got me good, Jen!"

Silence.

I should have seen it coming.

"I'm sorry, alright. A silly idea, I know. Always the fool, the clown, but can one of you let me out now, please?"

I'm trying to stay in control but feel my skin contracting around me. I'm not having fun. And I can't deny there's a little bit of anger building, too.

Jesus. That smell. Where's it coming from? Must be blowing in from outside.

With a clenched fist, I give the metal of the door a firm strike, temporarily disturbing the deathly quiet. "Jen!" Letting out another shudder, I snap my head around again. "We're going to be late for dinner!" Using my right shoulder this time, I give the door a firm nudge, but it doesn't give. "Jen, you've had your fun. Let me out!"

I wrap my fingers around the bars and push my nose through the gap. You could hear a pin drop. And the smell is getting worse, making my stomach churn.

Another breeze drifts through the window, licking at the back of my neck.

Holy shit. Holy fucking shit. "Help!"

I hear footsteps—from the corridor. Oh, thank Christ. "Hey, I'm in here. Leonard's cell!"

But a raucous noise from behind sets my heart pounding even faster—what sounds like metal scraping against stone. I snap my head around but only see the walls closing in as the grating continues. "Quickly! I think someone's in here with me." Squinting, I try and force the darkness to disperse, wisps of breath disappearing beyond the bars as the echoey footsteps continue to approach.

The scraping behind stops, replaced a haunting rattling noise drifting towards me from the corridor, a harsh metallic tune that offers no comfort.

What the fuck is going on?

Another cold compress wraps around my skin as the gust finds its way through. Against the side of the building and from above, I can hear the patter of heavy rain; I can smell it, too, but faint petrichor isn't enough to douse the ever-increasing odour of shit and piss. Another gust brings a high-pitched whistle that fails to die even as the draft on my neck abates.

It's coming from the corridor now, bringing an ominous dread.

"Eric's tune," a voice from behind me whispers. Breath held, I turn, but only diluted darkness awaits, and the initial of my first name in the wall, directly above LT's.

"Fuck no!" I bang against the metal. "Help! Help me!"

Wait—my phone. Urgently, I fumble it from my front pocket and begin typing. "What the fuck? What the fuck?" It doesn't even wake.

From the corridor, the whistling gets louder still.

And I see a silhouette through the bars. Broad shoulders, massive. They're wearing an angular hat and pushing something. A trolley?

This is insane, madness.

Out of the darkness, two more stocky figures appear behind the man's wide shoulders, and a different sort of scraping begins, menacingly loud. As the raucous harshness feeds down my bones, I press my face against the cold bars, searching for anything that might help alleviate the foreboding fear knotting my stomach.

"Clive on the left and Trevor on the right," the voice speaks from only inches behind. "Don't expect mercy from them."

Nobody there.

It's a tap-tap-tap feeding along the walls now and up and down my spine.

"The hell is this shit?"

"Playtime. What Eric calls it anyway."

I snap my head to the right, only to see the ever-approaching walls closer still.

Laughter emerges from the trio, but it isn't the jovial kind. They march in unison, black boots heavily crashing to the ground, metal apparatus on their trolley vibrating and shifting noisily.

"Help!" I scream. "Help!"

I can see the face of the whistler now. Eric? He sees mine, too, his lips curling to a snarl.

"My group," I croak. "I've got dinner reservations."

The three of them explode into raucous laughter. "Good one, Leonard," Eric mutters.

"Leonard? My name's not fucking Leonard; I'm Jake!"

"Jake with the dinner reservations," one of the two goons comments, setting them into another round of guffaws.

"My wallet," I utter, fumbling desperately at my back pocket. "Look! Here's my driver's license. That's me—Jake McCann! Look at the picture. Look at the fucking picture!"

"You're wasting your breath." That voice in my left ear.

"Open her up, Clive," Eric commands.

Stepping back from the door, I study Clive's face as he works at the bolts. I hear his rapid breathing and see the hungry anticipation behind the eyes that occasionally meet mine.

"There's been a huge mistake, Eric. I don't belong here!"

"The fuck did you just call me, you fucking maggot filth?"

"I just—"

"Get that fucking door open, Clive!"

My back against the damp wall, there's nowhere else to go. Cold rain runs down my neck, and it's making me sick with a longing to be outside again, to be free.

"My name is Jake."

Hinges moan as the metal door swings slowly open. It's impossibly cold, as though ice runs through my veins. I push my back against the stone as Trevor begins his approach, pounding the end of the bat into his open palm. "This might hurt a bit," he says.

"No, please! You've got the—"

A garbled yelp escapes my lips as pain explodes down my right arm. My entire right side lights up, nerve endings screaming towards a crescendo. "Please!" But Trevor growls in response, saliva spilling down his chin. The bat comes at me again, creating a soft thud as it connects with my wrist bone, sending searing pain up my arm that brings me to agonising tears. "Please, stop!"

"Is that what they said? Your victims, the families, the kids," Trevor spits.

"What are you fucking talking about?"

This time the swing comes low, and I'm too slow to get my arms out. The impact just misses a kneecap but forces my leg to buckle, and I let myself fall against the concrete bed, curled up like a fetus, bawling like a child.

"Strip him and tie him down!"

"Yes, boss."

Trevor rolls me onto my back and begins yanking at my shoes. I flail my legs in protest, but Clive quickly rushes in and pins me down.

"Please! I didn't do anything."

"I told them that, but it didn't help." That voice—to my right this time.

"He's here," I squeal. "Leonard, the one that you want; he's in here with us!"

My socks are next, followed by my pants and briefs. Buttons fly from my shirt as it's ripped open, and I'm left trembling against the cold concrete, not an ounce of dignity left. As Trevor reaches behind, taking the brown straps from Eric, I desperately try and wrestle free, but hands are on me, shoving down, searing pain exploding across my head as it falls against the stone.

"Leonard, tell them!"

Trevor goes to work, buckling the first strap tightly against my chest and pinning my arms. "This guy's crazier than a soup sandwich."

"They always do that," Eric snarls. "Blame it on the fucking voices. Turns my fucking stomach."

"No. I swear! Didn't you hear him—just then?"

"All I can hear, maggot, is a little boy that didn't get to suck on his momma's titty. Hurry up, Trevor!"

My legs are forced against the concrete at the snap of the second strap. The pain is an echo of what it was before, but it still torments, still throbs relentlessly. "I didn't do it! I didn't do it!"

"I pleaded, begged. Didn't stop them, though," Leonard's gravelly voice speaks from the corner of the room.

"There!" I scream. "He just spoke again. You must have heard that?"

"Enough of this bullshit," Eric says. "Trevor, get out."

"Boss."

Where are the others? Why haven't they come back for me? "What—what are you going to do?"

Eric brings his face close, hot air rushing from flared nostrils full of straggly grey hair. "I want you to confess."

I can't think. Fuck! None of this makes any sense. "My name is Jake. I came here with a group—on a tour of the prison. I have—dinner reservations."

Eric smiles and nods. "Dinner, yes." He reaches behind for the trolley, not taking his eyes from mine as he feels his way around the metal tray. "Ready for your first course?" he snarls.

"Help!"

Even confined, my body trembles relentlessly. So damn cold! My head is a world of pain and confusion; it's too much to process. I let out another deafening scream swallowed by the indifferent darkness. Warmth spreads down my thigh.

"Do you want me to gag him, boss?" Clive volunteers.

"No! I want to hear him sing."

"I didn't do anything! My name is Jake McCann. I live at 45 Ashbury Crescent. I'm an architect, working at—"

"Fuuuuuuuuuck!"

It feels like someone is playing strings with my fucking veins. Agony swells, magnificent red spilling from my chest. The smell of sweat, blood, and death hangs in the damp air, and there's no sign of salvation.

"Why did you do it?"

"I didn't!"

Eric digs the scalpel further in, and I let out an unworldly howl that only adds to the desolation. I can feel it in there, the cold blade scratching against my rawness. I bite down hard on my lip and bring my head back onto the concrete as he twists the tool, igniting a whole new level of torment. Turning, I retch, but only a croak emerges.

"Confess!" he spits at me, ripping the implement away and sending a spray of my blood splattering across the concrete.

"I'm not him!"

"You disgust me! What you fucking did. How many did you kill?"

"Already guilty, see. Made their mind," Leonard says from somewhere close.

"Why won't you listen? I'm not—No! What the fuck is that? No! No! No, don't, please! No!"

The pain is excruciating, a flash of lightning that ignites a fire inside of me. I'm screaming, crying, a ball of explosive pain and desperation. Blood begins to pool against my naked thigh as the cold metal works its way through tissue and bone, and helplessly, I listen to the crunching and tearing as Eric continues hacking at my index finger.

Music, distant and soft, begins to float across.

Pain continues to explore me, but it's dampening. The smell of steak is replacing blood and rust, and in the background, I can hear the superficial chatter of other patrons. "Can I take your order now, sir?" an underpaid waiter offers. I turn to Jen. She's wearing the green dress that I like.

Another wave of pain, fierce this time, and I'm back to a soundtrack of gristle and dripping water.

"Confess," Eric commands as he swipes my finger to the floor.

"My name is Jake! Fuuucccccck! Please, stop; I'm begging you."

I follow his finger to my chest and squirm as he slips it into the wound, moving it inside me, stoking at the fire that burns. I strain against the straps, but already the pain is beginning to dampen. I'm floating, carried on a cloud of darkness, staring down at myself. The three of them are beneath me, Eric lost in the moment, Trevor and Clive exchanging nervous glances as if it's getting too much even for them.

He removes his finger, and I'm back, writhing against the cold concrete once more. "Please, no more," I utter. "No more."

"What's your name?"

I open my mouth to speak. But I can't fucking think straight. Please let this end.

Eric moves his bloody finger towards my wound again. "Your name!"

"My name—my name is Leonard Thomas."

"See what pain can do?" Leonard whispers.

Eric gives out a sigh and drops his head. "At last, we're getting somewhere. The hacksaw, Clive."

"Perhaps we've done enough, Eric. I can't afford to lose my job—wife, kids, you know."

"Clive, you'll do as you're fucking told."

"Boss." Pale as the moon, he picks up the saw and tentatively offers it to Eric, as though expecting the guy to swallow his arms whole.

"I did it!" I scream. "I killed them all, okay. Please, just stop!"

"Now, that wasn't so hard, was it?" Eric rests the serrated blade against my thigh and gently begins to drag it across. "There was a family of four, lived near the old mill down Crescent Street. The best man at my wedding, Frank, his missus Jean, and my two goddaughters." He pushes the blade back with slightly more pressure this time.

"Please, I—"

"Trevor, I'm a man of my word, aren't I?"

"Boss."

"Give me the names of the two young girls, Leonard, and we'll call it a day. Simple as that. I just need to hear you say them."

"I—I don't know. Fuck. I—"

More pressure bites down on my leg.

"Going to need an answer, Len."

I can't even think of any fucking names. "Please don't do this."

"Out of time, I'm afraid."

"Fuuuuuuuuuuuuuck."

I'm lost, drowning in pain, impossible agony that's—

*

Ice cold water snaps my eyes open.

"Here he is," Eric comments, greeting me with a smile and a rusty knife. "We lost you there for a minute, Len. Now, one last chance. Their names."

As Eric steps forward and rests the blade against my neck, I order the steak, medium rare with the mushroom sauce and a glass of chianti, finally breaking into a sob.

"Rot in Hell, Leonard," Eric mutters.

*

I lurch forward, sucking in mouthfuls of air, my heart thumping violently. It's freezing, but I'm dripping in sweat. Voices echo outside.

"Jake!"

It's Jen.

"I'm in here, Jen!" Oh, thank Christ! Thank fucking, Christ. Overwhelming relief brings tears as I push myself from the bed, pain-free and with no sign of blood, all fingers present. More chatter emerges from the corridor, and the door swings open. "Jake."

"Jen, I'm so happy to—"

"He was in here before, Max. He was going to play a silly prank on Bec. I tried to talk him out of it, but he's as stubborn as a mule."

"I'm here, Jen!"

Max ducks his head into the cell. "I'm sure he can't be far."

"Maybe, but we've only been a minute, tops."

Jen shudders as my hands pass through her. What the fuck?

As Bev arrives in the doorway, Max coils his fingers around his cuffs. "Do you think he could be in a mood because you didn't follow through?"

"I don't know," Jen mutters. "There's always a chance. He's so up and down."

"Jen!" This is fucking insane. "Jen, I'm right here!"

Bec screws her face up, rubbing her arms as she steps back from the entrance. "Never known what you've seen in him; the man's a clown."

"Fuck you, Bec!"

"Jeez, it's freezing in here," Max says. "Come on. Perhaps he's on his way to the restaurant already?"

"He's not responding to my texts, though." She glances around the room, searching the darkness. If she looked closely enough, she'd see both my initials now etched in the wall, just under LT's. "I really don't like it in here," she says, giving a shiver.

"Come on," Bec says. "Let's go find him and give him a piece of our mind."

I try and follow, but an invisible forcefield stops me.

"Prison owns you now, son." More hot breath against my neck.

"Jen!" I scream. There's the familiar squeak of the hinges as the door swings shut, and helplessly, I listen to their footsteps fading into the distance. No, this can't be it. This isn't how it ends. I slam my fists against the metal and pull my face to the bars. "Jen!"

"You come into my home, lay on my bed. And all for a prank."

"Jen!"

"Well, I guess the joke's on you, kid."

I turn around to see him for the first time; an odd-looking man, tall and wiry, with a tuft of brittle grey hair and thick eyebrows almost meeting in the middle.

"April and Joy—the names of the kids, but it won't help. I think you saw that in his eyes."

"But—but the tour guide said you escaped."

"Just one of many cover-ups, Jake. The guards were as ungodly as the criminals. It's this place, you see; evil attracts evil, and the devil's always sniffing around for recruits."

The wind turns to a whistling that begins to surround us.

"Eric's tune," Leonard comments. "You'll get used to it."

I hear footsteps.

"Hell, I should be thanking you really, Leonard says. "I'm getting out, moving on. This cell is all yours."

The clatter of the trolley fills the corridor.

"Don't try and reason with them; they'll only make it worse. They just want their fill."

The tapping starts, running along the walls and into my spine.

"You get used to the pain, but the loneliness is a killer." He begins to fade. "Enjoy your stay at her Majesty's service."

The whistling gets louder.

SHE'S DEAD

She's dead.

Behind the eyes, I mean.

She moves the items over the barcode scanner with undeniable poetry, but it isn't rocket science. For a moment, I consider the idea of a checkout monkey. A little giggle sneaks out, but alas, nothing from—what is her name? Bethany. That's the name on the badge anyway. What a funny name that would be for a chimp. And then I think, what wouldn't be? Monica? Marge?

The explosion sends me to the floor, a thunderclap of shattered glass. I feel some of it pierce the right side of my body, but no pain registers. There's a ringing in my ears. Blood begins to seep through my crisp white shirt, and I wonder how I'll ever get it out.

I see someone slowly get up—a young man, perhaps in his twenties. He dusts himself off with his good hand. His other arm is on the floor next to a green basket. He glances around, and I follow his gaze across the debris. We catch sight of each other. I have never seen him before, yet I feel close to him.

My body starts to sting as the shock wears off. Slowly, I push myself up to see the conveyor belt covered in broken glass. I'll need to put that lettuce back.

I turn to face Bethany. Her face is a mess, cut to shreds by shards of glass that remain embedded in her skin; they sparkle in the evening sun like diamonds.

I start to move towards her, and she looks directly at me for the first time. Something isn't right. Shock can affect people in different ways, but her eyes are as dead as they were before. No sign of trauma. She turns back to the conveyor belt, picks up the juice, puts it through, and then roughly grabs the lettuce and asks if I want to change it for another.

The ringing in my ear starts to subside, and I can hear the sounds of people screaming and crying for help.

Bethany has just asked if I want to change my lettuce.

I scream at her then, "What's wrong with you?"

"It has a caterpillar on it," she replies sheepishly.

"Are you insane, woman?" I scream at her again.

For the first time, I see some fear in her eyes. It gives me some satisfaction.

Someone is pulling at my shirt, "Hey, buddy, are you okay?"

I turn around to see the guy from earlier, but any feeling of closeness has gone. He is unscathed, unmarked, and has both arms intact.

The manager approaches the next checkout with a broom and starts sweeping the broken jar from the floor.

It's happened again.

I need help. I've been back for three months, but it isn't getting any better. I'm beginning to wonder if it ever will.

I look towards the street outside and can see the enemy all around. The reflection in the window projects a much younger version of myself—gun in hand, full uniform—ready for action.

The end

ACKNOWLEDGEMENTS

A couple of quick ones.

Number one goes out to my mother for being my work's first reader and editor. Nothing gets past eagle-eye Jenny! Thanks, Mum.

To my wife, who has not only tolerated but also engaged with my incessant storytelling and idea-sharing. Her patience and understanding are truly remarkable.

A massive thank you to Ruth Anna Evans for reading my mind and creating one hell of a cover.

And to Tony Anuci, the publisher, for his instrumental role in breathing new life into the old hag.

Oh, and a huge thank you to top fans such as Paula Roxas, Kreszentia Uetz, Trish Wilson, and Leah Marcoux (to name just a couple) for helping keep me in the game.

Last but not least, I'd like to thank my writing pal, Erik Hanson, for always being there for a chinwag.

About The Author

Mark Towse is an English award-winning horror writer living in Australia. He would sell his soul to the devil or anyone buying if it meant he could write full-time. Alas, he left it very late to begin this journey, penning his first story since primary school at the ripe old age of forty-five. Since then, he's been published in over two hundred journals and anthologies, had his work made into full theatrical audio productions, and has penned fifteen novellas, including Mischief Night, Nana, Gone to the Dogs, 3:33, and Crows. Chasing The Dragon, his debut novel from Eerie River Publishing, was released in March 2024.